BURIED TEARS

Vivien Jones

Vivien Jones (nee Hackney) lives in Stoke-on-Trent, Staffordshire, England and is married with one daughter, a son-in-law and a grandson. She grew up in Goldenhill, Stoke-on-Trent and is the eldest of a family of six children: three girls and three boys.

DEDICATED TO

FAMILY

PAST, PRESENT AND FUTURE

TABLES OF CONTENTS

PROLOGUE

"Can you get the phone? Can somebody please get the phone" Wilf's daughter shouted. She rushed towards it and managed to grab the receiver before it stopped ringing.

"Hi Dad" she responded in surprise. Her Father never telephoned her at dinnertime. On this occasion however his call could not have waited. He needed her right then and there and roles and responsibilities were set to turn an almost full circle.

Does his wench wish that she hadn't reached the phone in time and, in desperation, her Father had telephoned another one of his children? If so then this book would never have been written and the tears and the truth contained within its pages would have remained buried forever.

As it was it was meant to be.

***

SIXTY-ONE YEARS EARLIER

Of his three brothers Kenneth was Wilf's comrade in arms, closest to him in age at nine, only two years his junior and therefore his second in command.

As the eldest child and simply because he had been born a boy Wilf carried an immense sense of duty and responsibility for all of his siblings but especially for Kenneth with whom he had an extraordinary bond.

It was not the question: 'What could I have done to have changed Kenneth's fate?' that haunted and tormented him but the truth contained within the buried answer.

CHAPTER ONE – A NORMAL DAY

SATURDAY 28 JUNE 1941

It was Saturday, but a washday nonetheless. Not an unusual occurrence but a vital necessity with three children and a three-month old babe needing a constant supply of nappy rags. There was also a pile of collars belonging to Mr Cooke, one of the few eligible bachelors in the village, that needed scrubbing, starching and ironing before he returned from his white-collared job at the transport office later that day. Sixpence was sixpence and that's what Nell would be paid if she finished his collars on time. The small kitchen was full of steam emanating from the boiler that was full to the brim with a wash of whites, a well-worn dolly peg and a scrubbing board.

"Shift ya bloody self before I knock ya block off" Nell bellowed as she pushed Wilf to one side. Nell was an awesome woman in every respect. Although quite small in stature rumour had it that she could have killed a man at ten paces with one lash of her tongue! Her well-rounded body, so shaped after the delivery of five live births and one dead 'un, had been concealed by a worse-for-wear wrap around pinafore and her full head of auburn hair was well and truly tucked under a cotton cloth turban.

"Take yoursen off and tack them bloody three with ya" she shouted into Wilf's face whilst, at the same time, she beckoned with a nod of her head towards his brothers Kenneth and Billy and his sister Alma. In unquestioning obedience, Wilf led the little pack outside and into the backyard.

"Now where shall we make for today?" Wilf questioned his three younger siblings who all looked much thinner after a full year of food rationing. Cheese had been reduced, yet again, to one ounce a week and was not enough to keep a mouse alive by Wilf's reckoning. 'So where could he find something for them to eat that they would not have to pay for?' he thought. 'The orchard, where else?' he answered himself in a millisecond. Just over the banks and up the hill the churchyard orchard would be bursting with small unripe apples, bitter to taste but food for hungry kids. Wilf's only hope was that the vicar didn't abort their raid by catching them red-handed and boxing their ears. He had already done that once too often for Wilf's liking.

What ragbags they all looked. It was after all a washday and their 'best' clothes were soaking in the tub. In features, Wilf and Kenneth were as different as chalk and cheese. Kenneth, almost ten, seemed small for his age and his blonde curly hair gleamed in the late June sunshine. On the other hand, Wilf almost twelve had strong, muscular features topped off with a mop of hair as black as the ace of spades. It was rumoured that Nellie 'musta' been with an Italian bloke to have had a lad so dark. But, like so many other things in the small village, it was only a rumour. Bill, her husband and dearest friend for over fifteen years, had the deepest, darkest of eyes with jet black hair to match so it was as plain as the nose on any bugger's face that Wilf favoured his Father in every respect. There was no doubting it. So Nell put the stories to bed with the rest of the gossip and there had been plenty of that during uncertain days of war and want.

Wilf confidently went up and down all the trees in the orchard as quick and as often as a fiddler's elbow in full rendition of Rimskey-Korsakov's Flight of the Bumblebee! He could be heard constantly egging Kenneth on, incessantly goading him and shouting instructions to 'follow his lead' and double daring him to do so. Eight-year old Alma, a sorry sight by any estimation, at best looked like a rag doll and at worst like a bag a muck tied up in the middle. Her matted and recently deloused hair was stuck to her head and clipped back off her face with two grips creating a side parting that looked, for all the world like a dog's back leg! She had been trying her hardest to pull young Billy, just four, along with her as she firmly grasped his hand in hers. In spite of her best efforts Billy was finding it a job and a half to keep up not least because his backside was hanging out of his oversized third-hand trousers that were held up and together with a piece of scruffy string. Once in the bottom half of the orchard Wilf lifted Kenneth up onto his shoulders to pluck a small apple off a high branch of a very old tree. It was to prove a blessing that Wilf had not known that this was to be the last time he would hold his brother's hand and lift him up in his strong almost twelve yet going on twenty-one-year old arms. Had he been allowed a glimpse, just a sneak preview, into the future then he would never have let his brother's hand slip from his own in a million and one years.

Finally, the four of them, three brothers and a sister, having laughed too much for too long, collapsed and plonked themselves down under the shade of a huge oak tree to scrunch their way through their plunder. They all knew, from past experience, that they would probably be two-double with bellyache later that night but like the rest of the country they were learning to live for the moment. As he looked at his siblings Wilf realised he regularly exceeded the demanding expectations associated with his role as the eldest boy and therefore felt proud and strangely satisfied with his timely provision of food and fun.

Wilf was a clever lad. He had passed the scholarship examination entrance test to attend the high school with grammar school status but due to the cost of the school's uniform and numerous essential extras, had been told, in no uncertain terms, that he would not be able to go. Only his Father, Bill, his Mother, Nell, and the four walls of the cramped living room ever heard the reasoning behind the decision to forego the offer of a place at the school. If they had little else they had their pride and would never have admitted the truth for their decision to any bugger. It was totally irrelevant that the Headmaster had earmarked Wilf as Prime Minister material subject to grasping the educational opportunity offered to him. His arithmetic and composition results in the entrance test were almost off the scale and he more than deserved the chance of fulfilling his innate latent potential. Deep in his heart however Wilf had always known such lofty ambitions were just 'pie in the sky' dreams and as such would always have been outside his grasp. No amount of fancy talk would ever have been able to change that especially since they didn't even own a pot to piss in.

For his part, when Wilf compared the grammar school opportunity, even embroidered with lofty expectations of grandeur, to the love he cherished for his family there was neither a competition nor a comparison. The offer of a grammar school education never really entered into the equation and came nowhere close to being a second best choice. Such resignations and responses borne in poverty and destitution remained with him for the rest of his life and his family became his first priority over and above his personal ambitions, possible achievements and probable acclaim. Anyway, he told himself, although he didn't care for the sentiment of the saying 'there was more than one way to skin a cat and he'd find another way of reachin' his unreachable stars. Just you wait and see he'd show 'em all' he concluded as he reluctantly relinquished his parliamentary dreams.

Wilf learned, at a very early age, how to sacrifice his aspirations for the love of his family. After all, in his 'book' he reasoned life would always be about honour, dignity and family. Therefore, whenever he needed to pass the high school and the pupils who graced its corridors he would take a deep breath, hold his head high, put his shoulders back, set his face like flint and walk past with as much pride as he could humanly muster. One day when he was passing the all girls' high school a catty smart-arsed wench, spotted him walking alongside the school railings; railings that served to keep her safely in and him safely out of the hallowed playground for more reasons than one. Although he never stopped walking Wilf saw her from the corner of his eye and immediately recognised her as one of his own class. In fact, he would have recognised 'Simple Sally' anywhere. She could never have totally disguised herself nor her humble heritage, even kitted out in a full high school uniform complete with an over-sized straw boater stuck on top of her bloody head. Wilf saw her just long enough to notice her place her hand firmly on top of her head to hold the over-sized boater in place. He found this most amusing since he thought the lass wouldn't need to be doing that for very much longer. According to all accounts, 'Sally's ego had grown that bloody fast and that big since starting grammar school that she'd soon need the biggest boater money could buy to fit her bloody big head in' he chuckled to himself at the thought of the scenario. Looking away he quickened his pace as Sally shouted after him as loud as she possibly could:

"We all know why you didn't go to the boys' grammar school Wilfrid Hackney. It's cuz you've got no arse in any of your trousers and your Father couldn't afford to put a uniform on ya back."

Wilf had not looked back that day but carried on walking as Sally's taunts and the laughter of her high school friends filled both the air and his ears before finding a resting place in his young heart and spirit. In an attempt to dowse the impact of her words he comforted himself with the saying that 'the cream always finds its way to the top; milk might get shaken up but in the end the cream always comes back to the top'. Deep in the depths of his being Wilf had somehow drawn comfort from the fact that he had won the right to be on the other side of the railings but learned from an early age that life was not solely about ability but also about social standing or the lack of it and may, in some circumstances, even boil down to what side of the sheets a bairn was born on. He discovered slowly that life had a raft of lessons to teach him from every situation he was destined to face and having been denied a grammar school education would prove to be the least significant of them all. In fact it would pale into insignificance.

Returning home from their little escapade Wilf and his siblings found the house empty. Nell was out and about with baby Terrence, probably returning Mr Cooke's collars in the hope of a sixpenny payment for prompt delivery of goods. Wilf had been crossing everything on the way home in the hope that his Mother would be out and in her absence spied his chance to create some fun and games for the little brood entrusted to his care.

During their time spent in the orchard Wilf spotted the biggest and ruddiest of all apples. It had obviously ripened well before its time but he thought the prize too regal to have selfishly and secretly munched his way through so without the others noticing he had yanked it off the branch and hidden it deep inside his trouser pocket. Although, on their journey home, the apple had started to burn a hole right through the lining of his pocket he managed to continue to savour the thought of it and carried it safely back in one piece. He had a special purpose in mind for it and once home immediately set about searching the kitchen drawers until he found a metal skewer and a length of rough brown string. 'He'd have to be quick' he thought as he kept one eye fixed on the apple and the other on the back gate half in anticipation and half in expectation of his Mother's return. He knew, only too well, he was skating on thin ice and running the risk of having his ears clipped again but he would do what he'd a mind to and no bugger would be able to stop him. He carefully tied one end of the string to the skewer and secured a double knot in the other end before he pushed the skewer and string straight through the middle of the apple and out the other side. He obviously devised this not so unique idea from having played conkers during the autumn months the year before. Once satisfied that the apple 'was going nowhere fast' he untied the end attached to the skewer enabling him to swing the apple round as fast as any champion conker player and much to the delight of the fascinated children. But this was only the start of the fun and a means to an end.

Because it had been a washday the drying rack, suspended from the ceiling in the middle room, was packed full of clothes but this did not prove an obstacle or a deterrent to the implementation of his new game. He quickly untied the ropes that held the wooden slatted rack close up to the ceiling until it slowly squeaked its way down. With one sweep of his hand all the clothes ended up in a pile on the floor and without further ado he quickly tied the string holding the apple to the centre slat in the middle of the rack and pulled the ropes up and down a few times in order to make slight adjustments. He allowed just enough string to enable even Billy, the smallest one, to be able to reach the apple and join in the game. Wilf, as usual, demonstrated the rules of the game first. Then, with their hands firmly tied behind their backs, Kenneth, Alma and Billy were allowed turns at trying to take a bite out of the swinging apple. It obviously refused to stay put and swung round for all its worth. All four of them fell about laughing until they thought their sides would burst. At one point however Kenneth stood back from the fun and games and just watched amazed and absorbed by the ingenuity of his brother. He had only admiration for him and would have trusted him with anything and everything including his life.

"What ya standing there for?" questioned Wilf. "Come on it's your turn. See how much, if any of it, you can get down your bloody neck".

In the end Wilf cut the apple down and divided it up as equally as he could. He was learning to waste nothing.

However tempting he had not cut a share of it for himself. Earlier, the thought of the apple had almost burnt a hole straight through his pocket but when the chips were down he divided it three ways instead of four and pretended to be enjoying his share along with the others. They all unanimously agreed that it was the best apple they had ever tasted in their entire lives! Whilst they continued to munch and laugh Wilf set about hiding the evidence of their game and returned the washing, in a fashion, back onto the rack.

Wilf always enjoyed treating his siblings even if it resulted in trouble for him in some way, shape or form. To treat them he often utilised some of the family's small store of food rations. Nell had a safe and secure hiding place for their allowances, one as safe as Fort Knox itself, or so she liked to think. Known as their 'tummy hole' it was a space above the top of the small pantry that could only be accessed by opening a hinged door in the ceiling. Nell had to use steps to reach and unlatch the wooden door in order to access their supplies and luckily for Wilf she did not find the time to conduct a stock-take very often. Just the night before the orchard raid while Nell and Bill were out visiting one of the local Public Outdoors Wilf, with hands and feet straddled either side of the panty walls walked easily up them, just like an 'incy wincey spider', to open the door and raid the contents of Nell's tummy hole. In it he found the remains of a tin of black treacle, together with some sugar stolen from various containers and a bit of powdered egg. The ingredients were ideal. He immediately started to blend them together on the stove in the small kitchen. All the time Kenneth, Alma and Billy were looking on, watching and waiting in anticipation as Wilf eventually boiled up his mixture amid very loud, excited and happy voices. Just as the concoction hit the right temperature Wilf shouted

"Pass me a cup a cowd (cold) waiter (water)" and, almost in unison, all three children jumped to and pandered to his command.

To cheers of excitement, Wilf let a droplet of the black liquid drip off the spoon and into one of the three odd and chipped cups of water being gripped as tight as one pound notes by Alma and Billy. One of the cups had no handle at all and Kenneth was therefore holding it all the more tightly. In fact, the family didn't own enough cups for them all to drink from at the same time so woe betide any of 'em if they broke one, even one with no handle on it.

"Solid as a rock" Wilf declared. "Quick get the owd (old) tray out and spread it with a lump a lard to stop it from stickin'". Kenneth, as if by magic, presented his big brother with an already highly greased receptacle. Slowly Wilf poured the black gold into the tray and just as it started to set he roughly scored it through with the end of a blunt knife. All four of them stood, watched and waited as the mixture slowly set and a 'watched kettle never boils' mentality became acutely evident. They each examined the rough cut marks and the size of the corresponding pieces all secretly and silently choosing which piece they wanted and were determined to 'bags'.

At last the waiting was over and Wilf, the big brother, hit the slab of black toffee on the underside of the tin with the back-end of the knife handle. Hands appeared from everywhere grabbing, fighting and 'bagsing' the biggest pieces. Eventually, they all sat down on the pegged rug in front of the empty fireplace under the dim light of the gas mantle and chomped their way through the home made treacle toffee treat.

"Who's the greatest?" Wilf asked Kenneth, Billy and Alma. "You are!" came the magnanimous unanimous reply.

That night Wilf managed, yet again, to provide another treat for his brothers and sister. They all had full bellies, were safe and warm and, as their big brother who always looked after them, he smiled with more than a tinge of relief and a sense of satisfaction. But, try as he may, Wilf did not have a 'cat in hell's chance' of stopping himself from worrying about the future. 'What might tomorrow bring for them?' he anxiously thought as he watched those he loved laughing, joking and devouring the ill gained slab of toffee. His experience of war years was filled with uncertain daylight hours and even more uncertain blackout nights. Fortunately he was unaware that the anxieties he felt were more than warranted and, if the truth were known, the extent of them belied the awfulness of all their futures. The most terrible of days and nights lurked around the corner waiting to overwhelm and consume them all. If only he had known the events of the week ahead. If only he had been allowed to peer into a crystal ball in order to have glimpsed what the future held then he would have given his very life to have changed its course and outcome.

Sadly, or mercifully, or both, Wilf was unable to see into the future and his part in it, but that joyous night he held his brothers and sister safe in the midst of a country torn apart by the ravages and insecurities of war as he attempted to cast his cares to the wind and join them in their unbridled fun.

CHAPTER TWO – A FATEFUL DAY

SATURDAY 5 JULY 1941

"Where's Kenneth? He should be home by now. Wilf, where is he?" Nellie screamed as she paced the floor with three-month-old Terrence firmly positioned in her arms. Her bairn hadn't settled since they had got back home after visiting a woman in Heath Street who was in maternal need. She wondered why on earth Terrence was being so grizzly. He had been crying on and off for most of the bloody day. She thought that the only good thing about bairns cryin' was that they needed to pee less and this reduced the number of nappy rags that needed washing. She half-wondered however if her bairn sensed that something was awry in the atmosphere pervading their small living space. Wilf definitely appeared uneasy as he kept looking at the face of the old clock positioned dead centre on the mantelpiece with its louder than normal rhythmic 'tick tock; tick tock'. He had been watching the time and hoping that Kenneth would rush in through the back gate, past the toilet and coalhouse and straight into the back kitchen before it reached four o'clock but it was a quarter past four and there was neither sight nor sound of him.

"Not seen him all day" Wilf sheepishly replied.

Nellie, the local makeshift midwife and 'layer-out' woman, had been out of the house for what seemed like most of the day and, as usual, without even thinking twice about it, had left Wilf in charge of the family.

When Nell was expecting Wilf she had no idea what happened at the birth of a baby and naively thought that her protruding belly button would open and the baby would be born through the centre of it. She had however on more than one occasion pondered about this concept especially since her belly felt big enough to burst. One day, whilst visiting her Mother and being just two weeks off her expected delivery date, she plucked up the courage to ask her straight out what to expect at the imminent birth of her first babe. Not wanting to appear totally ignorant and whilst proudly stroking her enormously round belly she said in an almost blasé off the cuff manner:

"Mother, will the doctor be called to stitch up the hole left in my tummy after the bairn is born?" The shocking truth hit her like a ten-ton weight and a bolt of lightning straight outta the bloody blue as her Mother simply and quite sternly replied:

"Dust know where it bloody went in?" "Yes" Nell coyly replied. "Well that's where it'll bloody come out!"

As a result of her own horrifying experience - ignorance certainly hadn't been bliss in this instance - Nell vowed that no other woman would be left in the dark in relation to pregnancy, birth and such female matters.

Driven with this determination she quite naturally evolved into the woman who was sent for at the birth of a baby and lost count of how many bairns she helped bring into the world and, by stark contrast, the amount of folk she washed and laid out ahead of their funerals. Being called to help with illness and death was something Nell did not carve out for herself. It was however generally assumed that because she knew what to do at births, especially difficult ones, she would also know what to do in any given illness or death. Anyway, Nell thought it fitting, even natural, that she was there when 'they' came into the world and was with 'em when they left it. As an off-shoot of her role she found herself unexpectedly respected by McGinty's the local undertakers and although she never received payment for any of her services she never refused to help anyone at a birth, during an illness, or after a death. It was not unusual then, with a constant list of home visits, for Nell to be out of the house and for Wilf to be left in charge in her stead. If he was honest about it, Wilf quite enjoyed the power and sway this assumed responsibility afforded him. That was unless something went wrong, something that would be his fault and his responsibility for the rest of his life.

Wilf had told Kenneth over and over again to keep well away from the Smith gang because they were always up to no good and although roguish the Hackney clan were angels when compared with literal thieves, robbers and scoundrels. Wilf, Kenneth and even young Billy always tipped their caps as a sign of respect to all members of the weaker sex regardless of their age. They never ever used their cheek or answered adults back no matter who told them off whether warranted or not. The Smiths, on the other hand, had no respect for any bugger and didn't even stand when the national anthem was played or sung. So, all in all, Wilf hoped that Kenneth had not gone off with the Smiths because he thought it a well-known fact that birds of a feather flocked together and it was therefore imperative not to be associated with thieves and robbers. In the light of this 'truth' all rum buggers with just a hint of a bad reputation were avoided at all costs and given a wide berth. In fact they were treated as if they had the plague itself and would contaminate anyone they touched or associated with. No, the surname Hackney would never be uttered in the same bloody breathe as that of the Smiths. Wilf would make damn sure of that.

The clock continued to tick more and more loudly as the minutes dragged by. Only Wilf appeared conscious of the slow loud 'tick tock' of the clock as the exaggerated sound reverberated through every cell in his body and with its every beat echoed accusingly: 'Where is he? He should be home! Where is he? He should be home!" Where is he? He should be home!"

Nell became increasingly worried and in her irritation and agitation flipped Wilf across his right ear with the back of her hand whilst, at the same time she shouted "Don't just sit there. Get and find him ya little bugger, get out and find ya brother and don't dare come bloody back until you've got him with ya".

17

With his ear swollen, stinging and red Wilf ran out into the backyard straddled his 'refurbished-in-a-fashion' bike before lifting it up and over the back gate and into the entry. He determined to peddle as fast as his local hero Tommy Godwin from Fenton who held the World Mileage Endurance record and whose name appeared in the Golden Book of Cycling. So Wilf peddled for all his worth an' like a bullet straight outta a bloody gun up and down Heath Street into Albert Street down over the banks and past Johnson's Garages. 'Where on earth could his brother be?' He brought his bike to a standstill using the topside of his feet and with his legs still straddled either side of the frame he raised both hands to his mouth and shouted his name over and over again:

"Kenneth", "Kenneth", "Kenneth" he yelled but Kenneth was nowhere to be seen and if he could hear his brother shouting his name he did not acknowledge it. The almost flat tyres on the wheels of Wilf's makeshift bike rhythmically hit the cobbled streets and he recognised, perhaps for the first time in his young life, the condemning voices of Guilt and Fear as they united to whisper in his ear:

"It'll be your fault", "It'll be your fault", "It'll be your fault" they taunted with every turn of the bike's wheels and in unison with the sound of the tyres as they moved over the cobbled street.

"Dear God, please please let me find him" he whispered to himself but even before the words left his lips he felt a lump as big as a ha'penny gobstopper grow bigger and bigger in his throat. It became so big that he thought it would choke him half to death. No matter how many times he swallowed his spit between his shouts for his brother the lump did not move. Fear tightened Her grip around his small throat and his heart felt as if it would burst right out of his small chest.

"Kenneth; Kenneth; Kenneth" he shouted without pausing. He would not dare to go home without his brother. His Mother would surely be true to her word and would kill him if he went back alone.

Wilf imagined, for a few brief minutes of respite, finding his brother playing Knock and Run down Taylor Street. He closed his eyes and pictured himself giving Kenneth a right mouthful firstly for playing Knock and Run and then for being shitty and holding a grudge against him; not to mention having worried him half to bloody death. Instinctively in his perfect picture he imagined himself with everything forgiven, letting Kenneth sit straddled on the handlebars of his old bike and carrying him safely home as he had so many times before. His heart therefore started to beat faster as he sped into Taylor Street half expecting to see him as true as he'd pictured him in his mind's eye but there was no string pulled across the road from door-knocker to knocker. No kids knocking, running off and falling about laughing when the doors adjacent to each other couldn't be opened due the tight stretch of string firmly attached to the knockers directly opposite each other. The string had been so taut that even twenty stone Joe at Number Ten was prevented more than once from opening his front door. But, turning into the street, there was no Kenneth or any of his friends to be seen. 'Perhaps he was playing shotties with the Smith gang at the bottom of the banks' he thought as Guilt and Fear travelled with him for what seemed like miles searching for his brother. Just before day started to give way to dusk Wilf very reluctantly and fearfully returned home with no brother in tow. No brother to sit on the handlebars of his rackety bike. No brother to sing along with him as they journeyed the roads together. He could not remember having felt so alone and so afraid.

Meanwhile, Alma and Billy were sent to weave their way through the cluster of homes and down the warren of streets of back-to-back terraces that helped make up the village of Golden Hill. The village was seven hundred feet above sea level and the highest point in the city bordered by Tunstall one of Arnold Bennett's Five Pottery Towns and Kidsgrove. The hill of gold was more than likely afforded its name due to the golden reflection of an abundance of gorse and buttercups, also known as gold cups, which glowed, especially in the summer sun, in the fields that covered the top of the hill. Some inhabitants liked to believe that real gold had once been found on the Hill but it was just another rumour and the gold in Golden Hill had little or nothing to do with gold in its truest sense. In and out of the ever-open doors the two children sauntered oblivious, for the time being, of the seriousness of the situation.

"Seen our Kenneth?" was the only question Alma asked as she pulled Billy alongside her. In more than one house they were told to look through the kids for themselves to see if their brother was among the six, eight, ten or more children crammed into every nook and cranny in the three small rooms that represented the ground floor of one of the claustrophobic terraces. The small rooms consisted of a parlour/front room, a middle/living room and the tiniest of back kitchens. All the rooms in the terrace including the two upstairs bedrooms were not big enough to 'swing a bloody cat in' let alone accommodate the biggest of families. But at least the houses had the luxury of their own toilet at the bottom of every backyard unlike the ones on top of the Hill where families still queued up to use the communal one.

In one house half way down the street children were playing aeroplanes under the middle room table whilst three or four of them were squashed onto an old armchair in the barest of living rooms. To own furniture, in any condition, was considered a luxury and in more than one house old tea chests and boxes were used in place of tables and chairs that were too expensive to buy. Alma was shocked to hear one child about the same age as herself crying because he had nowhere to sit and was even more shocked to hear his Mother's coarse instruction as she told him to 'stick your thumb up your arse and sit on your bloody elbow then'. In another home, three young children were almost submerged in the dolly tub being scrubbed with a brush in what remained of the washday water in the back kitchen. One glance in every house had been enough. Kenneth's blonde curly hair was so distinctive that any bugger could have picked him out immediately in a pack of a hundred and one bloody kids.

And so Alma who was holding on tight to Billy's hand pulled him along as they returned home to face Nell without any news of their brother.

The warmth of the mid-summer's day equalled the rising temperature in the house. Nell was trying to rock Terrence to sleep whilst soberly singing

"Show me the way to go home, I'm tired and I want to go to bed,
I had a little drink about an hour ago, and it's gone right to my head,
No matter where I roam, on land or sea or foam,
You can always hear me singing this song,
Show me the way to go home."

Suddenly and seemingly of its own accord, the back door blew open and an uneasy hush weaved its way through the house and settled like a thick heavy blanket over the small two up and two and a half down. It felt like the uncanny feeling of calm experienced just before a storm and generally followed by an almighty bang of thunder. For the first time that day Nell too sensed the presence of Fear. She had found a way into her home and her cloak was forming an oppressive blanket as She lingered in the wings waiting for the storm and the thunder and lightning to start. Nell hoped that on this occasion her intuition, her gut feeling, her inner witness, would be wrong. Over the last year she had known that 'lightning' was on its way before the sirens sounded out their warning of a blitz. This instinct allowed herself and her family a little extra valuable time. They either ran to the brick air raid shelter with its concrete roof at the bottom of Albert Street or crawled into their own cage like one in their front room. But in that awful moment of intuition Nell's biggest fear was that there would be no shelter strong enough to shield and protect them from the fearful storm that she sensed was brewing. She shivered as she felt someone walk straight over her grave and there was no mistaking that feeling. Nell had a real sense for such things having had many experiences before the tempests of heavy and frequent bombing raids, not to mention her sixth sense when it came to the dead and dying. Her only uncertainty at that moment in time was:

'Had Fear come alone or had one of her never ending entourage come with her'? Nell knew that Fear never normally worked alone and had a huge cohort of counterparts each one of them as terrible, in their own unique way, as the next. On this day, this very day, Charon, the ferryman, stood alongside Her as if waiting for a payment to cross the river and if Nell, with her sharp sixth sense, was aware of Him she refused to give him any credence.

Only time would tell the truth of it and Nell thought that if she kept herself busy and ignored her strong sense of foreboding then everything would 'come out in the wash' and Kenneth would be home soon for his tripe and onion supper. She should have known better.

CHAPTER THREE - MISSING

As was his custom on a Saturday afternoon, Bill and the majority of working class men who lived in the village went straight into one the many pubs on the Hill for a pint or two of best bitter at the end of their day's shift. Very few of them ever actually tasted their first pint simply because it 'went down in one and never touched the sides' let alone a single taste bud. As normal, the bar was full to capacity. Groups of men were huddled around small round tables with cast iron legs and solid wooden tops playing all manner of card games for all manner of wagers. Bill, to Nell's delight, had won many a dead rabbit in one of the free-for-all card games. Providing a rabbit stew feast for the family was a treat and a half. On another table one man, thick in coal dust, knocked the edge of a domino in frustration on the well-worn table top as an indication to the other players that he was unable to 'go' and therefore missed a turn. He tried to conceal his irritation but the whites of his eyes grew wider and, coupled with his solitary front tooth, gleamed against the backdrop of black soot and coal dust that covered his face. The atmosphere was thick with cigarette smoke and the smell of beer and sweat merged to fill the air, nostrils and lungs of everyone in the pub. They congregated in an attempt to revive not only their bodies but also their spirits at the end of long hard shifts worked in local iron and steel factories or the deepest and darkest of mine shafts.

Bill was standing up, taking everything in as he leaned by the door to the back-way. He was discussing things of little or no importance, just making small talk, with one of his many mates when a runner, flushed and out of breath, appeared at the outdoor hatch to the public bar.

Children of all ages were sent on errands to the outdoor hatch. Some to have empty bottles or jugs filled up with mild beer at 5d a pint to carry out to family and neighbours who preferred, for one reason or another, to drink at home. If the beer was for a woman then the runner would normally be under strict instructions not to tell anybody who it was for especially if the family were Methodists. Licensees were extra vigilant when selling beer for consumption off the premises especially to children on errands and especially if they wanted to avoid a hefty fine of two pounds. They were required by law to ensure that beer supplied to children under fourteen had been sealed by applying a paper, wax or purpose made red seal to the vessel used. A child over fourteen could however legally be sold beer for consumption off the premises without the use of a cork or any seal whatsoever and therefore proved the most popular errand runners to public houses.

The outdoor hatch in the Horse and Jockey looked straight into the back of the bar with its shiny brass pumps only hidden by the shapely backs of the barmaids, who never stopped pulling pints unless the barrels ran dry. On the other side of the bar men were standing, as usual, two double, waiting not so patiently to be served.

Jack, a young errand runner of thirteen, arrived at the outdoor hatch. He had been commissioned by Nell to run into all the pubs on the village to look for Bill and when he found him to pass on an important message to him. Jack was renowned for being a sensible errand boy and one who could be trusted and relied upon to do whatever was asked of him. Because of this he was well known by the landlords in every one of the many pubs in the village. Most of them just filled his empty bottles with beer without arsing about with a seal simply because Jack looked and acted older than the magic fourteen years of age. On this occasion however Jack was not fetching beer for any of the women or men who regularly used his services for a ha'penny a time. Today he had been sent on a very different mission altogether. Without waiting for his turn or to be asked how old he was or what vessel he wanted filling Jack shouted out as loud as he could above the noise and over the heads of the buxom bar maids:

"Is Bill Hackney in yer?" There were almost as many pubs in the village as shops and because Jack had already run into the Wheatsheaf and the Swan he was more than relieved to hear an almost immediate response:

"Aye, what's want? What's up?" Bill replied in disbelief. "Thait wanted at wome. Thy Kenneth's missing!" the lad shouted. 'Mission accomplished' Jack thought to himself. He could make his way straight home and turn his ha'penny over to his Mother to put with the family's income giving 'em at least two ha'pennies to rub together. 'After all', he concluded. 'There was nothing more for him to do for his money.' That was all Mrs Hackney had told him to do and say when he found her man. 'He was wanted at wome cuz Kenneth was missing' and that was as much as he knew, nothing more or nothing less. So he delivered the simple message in double quick time, an unexpected bonus, and gratefully pocketed the payment. Jack had his own suspicions about the missin' lad and thought he would soon turn up because he had seen him playing Hide and Seek with some other boys just a couple of hours earlier on the banks behind the garages. He had deliberately not volunteered the information to Mrs Hackney and did well to hold his tongue for fear of shooting himself in the foot, nullifying the need for an errand and his payment for it. A ha'penny went a long way in the family's kitty and anyway he always minded himself with his own bloody business especially when he was sent on secret errands.

Although in the middle of his pint Bill downed the remainder of it in one hit, turned his back on the pub and started walking through the back streets towards his home. Nothing ever disturbed the master of the house from his beer especially since there was a shortage of it as a result of the recent fuel crisis and transport problems. Runners were only normally sent to search out the men of the village in extreme emergencies and it had never been known for Nell to send for Bill in all their years of marriage not even when she was in labour over their last bairn. Because of this Bill immediately sensed the seriousness of the situation and realised that Nell must have been worried sick to have sent a runner for him.

Bill was over six feet tall, a good-looking man with strong features and even stronger moral values. He was a foreman at the local iron and steel foundry and had been hard pressed to keep up with demand and production during uncertain war days, months and years. Even though he was regarded as 'one of the boys' Bill didn't like to see men sitting around playing cards when they should have been producing iron and steel. Blackouts had taken their toll on production but Bill, who had been a soldier in the war that should have ended all wars, was still determined to serve his King and country in any way he could and if that meant being regarded as a 'bossy bugger' then so be it. Because of his reliability and moral values Bill was highly respected by management and it was rumoured that sooner or later he would make a white-collared worker. His pace quickened as he approached his home.

'Surely his little 'un would be home by now' he thought to himself. 'Surely there'd been no reason to have sent a runner into all the pubs in the village. Runners were only sent in emergencies and he could count on one hand how many times he had known it happen. Surely this hullabaloo would prove totally unnecessary and totally unwarranted' Bill concluded as he walked through the back door of his small house.

His home seemed empty. It felt cold on a late mid-summer's afternoon. Kenneth wasn't there. One sweep, one scan of the house was enough for Bill to have determined that much. Terrence, thankfully asleep, was in the bottom drawer of the tallboy positioned in the corner of the middle room. Nell was rocking backwards and forwards in the old rocker with an increased sense of foreboding overshadowing her. She refused to voice her apprehensions just in case Fear herself made her wildest and worst imaginations turn into a living nightmare. She refused to speak them out and that way they would not come true. She would not; she dare not tempt Fate as she looked up at her man, her Bill, in disbelief.

Wilf, back empty-handed from his cycle circuits, continued to act sheepishly and could not, for love nor money, keep himself still as he jumped around the house 'like a cat on a hot tin roof'. Alma sat quietly on the makeshift ledge under the windowsill with her arm gently placed around Billy who was swinging his legs in mid-air in time with the ticking of the mantelpiece clock. In spite of the warmth of the late afternoon every person in the house sensed a distinct change in temperature as Fear extended her icy fingers and gently, but very deliberately, exhaled her caustic breath into the entire room. She had her own unique way of extracting oxygen from the atmosphere in order to leave her prey gasping for breath.

Before the man of the house was able to take full charge of the situation a number of men, who had followed hot on Bill's heels from the Horse and Jockey appeared at the bottom of his backyard. Jack, the messenger, had shouted loud enough to be heard by more than one pair of ears and the news had spread like wild fire around the public bar. The men, the volunteers, were all still dressed in their working clothes. Often classified as common men they were nonetheless a group of men who proved, every day of their lives, to be the salt of the earth. Some were covered from head to toe in the blackest of coal dust. Many had worked a double-shift, not only for the extra money, but in order to raise production levels which had been drastically reduced as younger men turned their backs on the industries to enlist and serve their country on the battlefields. Fewer men had been conscripted from the village than in other areas of the country because the Hill had been identified as an industrial area. A large majority of the village's men had therefore secured employment in reserved occupations earmarked as being vital to the war effort. Although deadbeat and fit for nothing they pulled themselves up by their bootlaces and united as one to help search for the lad. There were too many children to count in the village and whilst it was perfectly acceptable for parents 'not to spare the rod for fear of spoiling the child', if one of them was hurt outside their own home, or, if they suffered an accident or a serious illness of any type then the village moved with the strength of an army to protect its young. A lad, one of their lads, had been reported missin'. Kenneth, the blonde curly haired un, and the search for him had started.

Nell tried to remember when she had last seen Kenneth and recalled it was about noon when the sun was at its highest that she spotted him on the corner of Church Street and High Street just outside Brown's sweet shop with three or four playmates. She remembered calling to him: 'Be in by three' but did not slow her determined pace one fraction. In fact, in her eagerness to reach her destination she did not even pause but quickened her stride as she turned her head and shouted her instruction towards him whilst, at the same time, she repositioned Terrence in her arms.

Nell had however more than slowed her pace as she neared her destination and looked over her shoulder several times to ensure that no bugger had followed her. She quickly scanned the windows of the houses on either side of the road to check for any movement behind the shabby net and blackout curtains before slipping unseen into a doorway halfway down Heath Street. The women in the village trusted Nell implicitly with their deepest secrets, fears and medical problems and especially those connected with pregnancy and childbirth. Many of the women had rolled up their sleeves to work in essential jobs while men who had never travelled farther than the next village were sent to serve their country abroad. Women filled the gap that this exodus created and became employees at the local munitions factory or conductresses on the tram service that ran out of track at the top of the Hill. Some women experienced an unexpected knock on effect as a result of their liberation from the kitchen sink and started to enjoy a taste of independence that they had never thought possible before the outbreak of war. They realised they were capable of providing a living for themselves and started to 'let their hair down' and enjoy life to the full in every respect and in defiance of the threat of invasion. They often sought Nell's advice on covert relationships and how to avoid becoming pregnant as a consequence of them. They trusted that she would never divulge their confidences even if it resulted in being misunderstood herself. But how could Nell possibly have known that family history and her own broken heart would condemn her for being, on that July day, in the wrong place at the wrong time? Nell, in normal circumstances, had an intuition for such things but on that most fateful of days she was preoccupied and had not given the situation on the corner of Church Street a second thought or a moment's concern as, without hesitating, she hurried past her little lad and his pals.

Children played without fear on the Hill and confidently wandered outside its boundaries in order to pat the backs of horses as they pulled industrial barges alongside the array of canal paths and tunnels. They often played together for hours on the barren banks and raised hills of the village pretending to be Robin Hood or Ivanhoe or making camps deep within the forested areas of Wilson's Wood playing cowboys and Indians. Everyone knew everyone else and parents expressed confidence and security in the knowledge that there was 'an all for one, and one for all' ethos and culture ingrained into the strong foundations of community life.

Anyway, Nell mused, Wilf was her big 'un and she always left him in charge in her stead even though, on this occasion, she had deliberately not told him where to find her if the need arose. After all it was a normal Saturday and there had never been any need for concern before. So how could Nell possibly have known that the briefest of instructions shouted to Kenneth as she hurried swiftly past him on that fateful Saturday would be the last words she uttered to him this side of heaven? Had she been more in tune with her senses, had she not been so preoccupied, had she not been in the wrong place at the wrong time then she would have vehemently fought back Fate Himself and His darkest, most dreadful companion Death for having dared to cast their shadows over her blonde curly haired son. 'It was not his time, his number could not have been up and been called out. How could it possibly have been? He was only nine years of age' she reasoned as thoughts tumbled through her troubled mind.

Before Bill went out to his small group of drinking partners who had faithfully followed him home and whose inquisitive heads were peering over the top of the entry gate, all six foot two of him stooped down until he came eye to eye with Wilf.

"When and where did you last see Kenneth son?" he gently asked.

By this time Wilf felt overwhelmed by the suffocating presence of Fear as She used her tourniquet to firmly tighten Her stranglehold on him. He could barely breathe as his swollen tongue stuck to the roof of his dry as a bone mouth as his Father looked longingly at him. For a second or two Wilf was temporarily paralysed and so petrified that he could not speak in order to tell his Father the truth. He had been told often enough and therefore believed without question, that in all circumstances 'honesty was always the best policy' and so he desperately wanted to tell his Father the truth. In any case, had he not wanted to tell the truth, he would never have been able to lie to the eyes of the man he loved and respected more than any other human being on the planet but before he could answer Nell jumped into the pregnant pause

"It was dinner time, about twelve when I saw him on the corner of Church Street. I was on my travels with Terrence around and about the village. I saw him last; he was with three or four other lads and a wench, yes, I think there was a wench with 'em as well" she confidently declared. Bill stood bolt upright as if a rod of iron had been invisibly forced down his strong backbone. "Bloody hell!" he said. "It's just gone half-past six!"

Wilf was glad that he could not see his Mother's face. Glad his Father's eyes were no longer searching his soul, glad that the attention had been transferred from him to his Mother as his Father asked further questions and his Mother duly answered them in the briefest of interrogations.

With the events clearer in his mind Bill went out through the back kitchen door, down the yard and outside the gate to relay the latest information to his own personal army of volunteers. After some deliberations everyone agreed to separate and search on foot in different directions for Kenneth. They thought it a good idea to conduct a check of all the homes on the Hill who had boys of a similar age to Kenneth because Nell, perhaps in her eagerness not to be seen, had not noticed who the other young boys were and only recalled that they were similar in both height and age to Kenneth.

'With so many children in the village this was going to be a long night' Bill thought to himself. The small party of men split up and started the search while Bill went back into the house to go over the details of Kenneth's last known whereabouts one more time with his Nell.

CHAPTER FOUR –

A WILD GOOSE CHASE

Bill didn't know how the local police station got to hear about their unfortunate state of affairs but in response to an impudent knock on his front door, Bill found himself confronted by a young constable dressed in a full police uniform crowned with the biggest blue helmet imaginable.

"We've received a report that one of your children is missing, sir" the PC confidently declared whilst looking straight into Bill's face.

Policemen were feared and revered almost on a par with God Himself in Golden Hill and therefore commanded respect from every quarter. People of the village almost nonchalantly politely played along with police procedure in the hope of seeing the back of 'em as soon as possible. The young Police Officer had plodded his way down the streets in response to a formal report of a missing child and on the orders of Sergeant Pierce. On his way down he walked past innumerable young children playing outside the terraces on dirty-grey moth-eaten itchy woollen blankets in the hope of absorbing the last rays of July sunshine. Before the Officer's huge shadow had fallen across any of them they had all been swept up, together with their worse-for-wear toys, and taken inside. Doors firmly slammed and locked behind them as if protecting them from some archenemy. Although respected by the close-knit neighbourhood there was little trust of the prying police force. In fact, although highly revered the unanimous consensus was that policemen were not to be trusted 'farther than you could spit or bloody throw 'em'.

As the doors all firmly locked out the presence of the law the cobbled streets became still and deathly quiet. An eerie hush and an uncanny calm joined forces with Fear Herself as She spread her net as wide as possible in an all out attempt to engulf and stifle the small community.

At almost seven o'clock it was a good twelve hours since the family had enjoyed a toast and drippin' breakfast prepared on the open fire with the elongated toasting fork hand-made for the job by Bill. They had moved to the house on the Hill from the Abbey in late 1939, mainly because it had running water at the turn of a tap thereby eliminating the need to queue at the standpipe with buckets and bowels to fill to the brim with water before struggling to carry them home. The standpipe had only been turned on for a few hours a day and many a child suffered a thick ear for having spilt too much of the liquid gold whilst trying their utmost to carry it safely back. Try as they may however the water still splashed and splurged its way over the sides of the overfull receptacles amidst the hustle and bustle of the conglomeration around the standpipe. Fresh running water on the Hill proved to be an absolute luxury-and-a-half and the family lapped it up! A big downside of the move however was the unexpected fear of using the open fire to cook food on. What the family had not known at the time of the move was the fact that it wasn't just water that was running in the house. It had an infestation of cockroaches that were bigger in every way than anything Bill had ever seen in his life and the big black buggers lived behind the warmth of the open fireplace. Although the 'roaches kept themselves hidden during daylight hours at night the fireplace and hearth became alive with them. A living mass of shiny black beetles of the worst possible kind! When the house was asleep, Bill woke Wilf up to help him eradicate the infestation by shovelling the buggers up and hurling them, alive, onto the huge open fire. There were so many 'roaches that shovelling 'em up ten to the dozen had only made headway against them until the living black mass engulfed and extinguished the fire that was stoked half way up the chimney. Eventually, over many weeks, and continuous nights of shovelling, the flames started to win the fight and together with every treatment in the book, the house was declared clean and the fire safe to cook on. This came as a huge relief to Nell as it removed the dread of serving up toasted 'roaches as a side dish without having noticed them! Vermin were a constant battle in the close-knit terraces. They travelled through the back-to-back walls and fireplaces and if one house had them then before very long the whole street had them. The terraced community shared everything, including cockroaches and vermin.

As usual, Bill had quietly left for work at 5am that morning. Everyone else in the house was expected to be up and dressed by 7am at the very latest. If any bugger dared to remain in bed after roll call then Nell threatened to send for the undertakers to come and lay 'em out. After all, she reasoned they must have been bloody dead not to be up and dressed at such a late hour. Her supposition behind this rule was:

'there was nowt to be had in bed after seven in a mornin' 'cept bed sores and babies'. So everyone under her roof was up every day of the week and passed inspection by seven at the very latest. None of her brood would ever be accused of eatin' the bread of idle sods.

Bill led the young policeman straight through the parlour and into the already overcrowded middle room as if to conceal him from the outside world. Nell, Wilf, Alma, Billy and Fear turned in unison to stare at him. PC Shaw commanded the room's full attention and yet seemed awkward, ill at ease, as he stood dumb struck for more than a few seconds but seconds that felt like hours to his captive audience. His presence, nonetheless, could only be described as awesome.

"Please sit down" Bill said pointing to a high backed chair. "Move over, our Alma and make room for PC... what did you say your name was?"

"Shaw. PC Shaw" he replied with more than half a stutter as he gingerly positioned himself uncomfortably on the edge of the old high-backed chair and tried as inconspicuously as he could to loosen the stud that attached his stiffly starched collar to his shirt.

Everything seemed upside down, back to front and inside out as Wilf wished with all his heart he could turn the hands of the mantelpiece clock with its condemning loud tick back in time. He wondered half petrified to death, if the Policeman had come to arrest him. 'But nobody knew what he had done, did they?' he tried to reassure himself. His heart however continued to pound and move faster than the rhythm of a weaver's shuttle. His hands were clammy and sticky and his head spun round as blood pulsated and throbbed through every vein in his young body and mind. Fear, watching from the shadows instinctively curled her lips at both corners creating the most sickening and satirical of smiles. She liked to capture her prey young, the younger the better. Once in her grasp she could feed off them for a lifetime. She could stifle and suffocate them just long enough to weaken and control them as she endeavoured to limit their purposes and abort their destinies in life. Wilf looked on helplessly as if watching the dawdling drawl of a film running in the slowest of motions at the village picture palace. He could not believe or equate to what was happening within the four walls of their middle room. He watched as the Policeman steadily unfastened the shiny button on the top pocket of his jacket uniform and in a deliberate manner extracted a small pocket notebook and pencil. He coughed into the silence to clear his throat and enable him to adopt an official tone of voice. "Now when was your lad last seen?" he probed. "Kenneth, is it?"

"Erm, erm, I haven't seen him all day" Wilf blurted out although the question had not been directed towards him. "Nell saw him last" Bill offered. "On the corner of Church Street and High Street with a couple of other lads; told him to be in by three, she did, by three". Before the questioning progressed any further Sam Squires and Archie Brown, two of the men in Bill's small search party of volunteers, appeared at the bottom of the yard and shouted over the top of the back gate: "We've got news. Good news" Sammy, the biggest and dirtiest of the two of them cheerfully declared.

"Stanley Black, Joe's youngest lad has been playin' with your Kenneth today. He was with him in Wilson's Wood only a couple a hours ago" Archie piped up.

Immediately PC Shaw snapped his notebook shut as if disgusted. He thought there would be a simple explanation for the late return of the lad. There was always a simple solution in these types of situations. He was normally sent on wild goose chases by his Sergeant and had only been ordered on this one because the local busybody, Annie Jones, had reported the lad missing despite the fact that it was none of her bloody business in the first place.

'Been better if she'd have kept her big nose out of where it didn't belong' he thought to himself as he considered the extra paperwork and legwork she had caused him. 'Yes, nothing but a cheeky blighter who looked as if she'd been dragged through a bloody hedge backwards an' she was wearing red and green together and every bugger knew that red and green should never be seen except upon a fool' he silently summarised as he recalled the logging down of the incident at the station desk earlier that day.

Annie had been in such a hurry to get to the station, before anyone else beat her to it that she turned up at the desk with a head full of clips tucked under a dark brown hair net that had more big holes in it than mesh. She thought the young policeman might be on duty so decided the occasion warranted the application of rouge and lipstick. Before leaving her house she had generously applied rich ruby tones to her cheeks and lips before donning a tight scarlet jumper. Her even tighter green skirt was half way up her bloody backside revealing the tops of her seamed stockings. She was not a very pretty sight and PC Shaw was not impressed in any way shape or form by her appearance. He was of the opinion that 'there was no fool like an old fool' and she was a bloody fool an' a half in more ways than one according to local reports. He didn't know what the attraction was, but Annie always seemed to enjoy visiting the station and rushed to tell him anything and everything she got to hear about often before anything had actually happened. Yet again, she had jumped the gun in her reporting of a blonde curly haired lad who had supposedly gone missing.

"Just thought you should know", she'd concluded having not stopped to take a breath as she elaborated and exaggerated the story of the missing boy. She just loved a bit of gossip did Annie. In PC Shaw's opinion, although it had rarely been sought or asked for since his appointment eighteen months before, she had made a mountain out of a bloody molehill yet again. He really wanted to formally report that Annie Jones was as daft as brush and a tile short of a full roof but that would definitely have blotted his copy book with the Sergeant so he quietly accepted that there was nothing quite as funny as folk.

'What a waste of time' the young PC concluded. He'd walked all the way down the Hill to question the lad's parents only to discover that the whole fiasco was nothing more than a false alarm and a fart in a colander. He would still have to follow up his enquiries and he'd probably end up writing another long and useless report to file away with the rest of them. He stood up to leave. He expected to be on duty 'til at least ten o'clock that night and it looked like being a very long shift. He just knew it. He could feel it in his water.

Wilf however breathed an unnoticed sigh of relief as Fear immediately released Her grip of his throat. He had circled the edge of Wilson's Wood during his bike search but hadn't actually ventured inside it on foot. 'Bet ten to one he's hiding in there still grieved with me' he thought. 'He can be a bugger for holding a grudge can our lad. He might even have heard me shouting his name and hidden deliberately.' Thoughts tumbled through his mind. He could however barely contain his relief and excitement. 'His brother would soon be home. At worst, perhaps he'd fallen and hurt himself. Didn't he have to regularly give him a leg up into the biggest trees in the grounds of the orchard?' he recalled as his mind raced on and on. 'Hadn't he goaded him, dared him to go up higher? Bet he'd fallen out of a big old oak in Wilson's Wood' he thought. 'Bet he had.' The words rushed through his mind drawing pictures of his brother with a broken leg or ankle but safe and well and that was the only important thing in his small but vital world. Even if the Jerries bombed 'em that night it wouldn't matter one iota to him just as long as Kenneth, his brother, was in the Morrison shelter with them where they would all be safe and sound. Snug as bugs in rugs. 'Better to be in there all together' he thought 'especially if the rumour was true that the communal shelter at the bottom of Albert Street was no bloody good cuz it hadn't got an ounce a cement in its concrete!' Wilf thought that the rumour was probably just another bit of propaganda whatever propaganda was. In any case he was glad of it whatever it was if it kept 'em outta the communal shelter. He didn't care for using a steel drum as a toilet an' squashing on a bunk bed with half a dozen others however heavy the blitz was.

On his way back to the station PC Shaw decided to kill some time by visiting the Blacks in Queen Street. He knew the family well. They managed to keep their noses clean in spite of the fact that it was strongly suspected that they conducted a fair trade in black market contraband. True to form, and in immediate response to his knock on the door the bobby heard a good deal of hustling and bustling taking place before the door was eventually opened by a very flustered and flummoxed Mrs Black.

"Evening, Mrs Black. Could I have a word with your Stanley please? It won't take a minute or two. I understand he's been playing with Kenneth Hackney today". Betty Black screwed up her face as if there was a bad smell underneath it and folded her arms across her broad chest before she reluctantly beckoned him over her front step.

PC Shaw had often seen Stanley playing in the street with other boys of his age as he conducted his village circuits. His boots knew every inch of Golden Hill. Whatever mischief or tricks the boys were up to the sight of his police uniform was enough to stop 'em dead in their tracks and make 'em disappear as fast as rats down drainpipes. The young constable would secretly have liked to join the children in their fun and games especially footie or shotties but he would never have dared remove his helmet and let his hair down. It would have proved more than his job was worth, not to mention adding to his Sergeant's disdain of him. He needed to work hard and keep his nose clean to stay well and truly on his Sergeant's good side at all costs and, if possible, impress him at every twist and turn. 'Anyway he'd have this one sorted out and filed away just as fast as you could say Jack Robinson' he smugly thought and still make it back to the station in time for his tea break and his tuppence ha'penny Cadbury's chocolate bar followed by a few hours of peace and quiet. If it did prove to be a long night then he would be able to put his feet up and make it a comfortable one. Time and history were set to prove how very wrong the assumptions of a young inexperienced Police Constable could be.

CHAPTER FIVE –

A HIDING FOR NOTHING

As soon as the door closed behind PC Shaw a lighter breeze blew into the small living room. The air and atmosphere seemed brighter as Hope rekindled her flame.

'He'd be back soon. He'd be back soon. He'd be back soon.' Wilf rhythmically pondered over and over in perfect time with the endless ticking of the old clock in the centre of the mantelpiece. 'Yes, Kenneth would be back home fit and well soon' he assured himself.

"Right you three let's be having ya. It's eight o'clock. Your hands and faces can go without a cat lick tonight so get ya selves up them wooden hills to bed and don't dilly dally on the way" Nell almost sang with a lilt in her voice and half a smile across her face. At the same time, like a shepherdess, she gathered her children together, opened the door to the bottom of the stairs and herded her lambs through it.

She couldn't put her finger on it but Nell was unable to shake off the sense of dread resting deep in the pit of her stomach. It felt as heavy as the Stafford knot itself which it was rumoured had once been used to hang three criminals at the same time by using the three loops that formed the famous knot. She thought it a dreadful thing to even half imagine and therefore refused to believe it, just like she refused to believe the overbearing feeling of doom that felt heavier than a hundred and one bloody knots around her neck. Nothing about the events of the day made an ounce of sense to her. 'If it was true that Stanley Black had been playing with Kenneth in Wilson's Wood then why was Stan back at home and Kenneth wasn't? Not like them at all', she reasoned. 'The lads normally stuck together unless there'd been a falling-out between 'em. They could be buggers for that. No, something wasn't right. It didn't add up at all' an' she felt as sick as a dog about it.

There were only two bedrooms in the small terraced house and all four children slept in one bed in the back room over the top of the small middle room underneath. Generally, all the children went up to bed together. This enabled them to find their preferred top to toe places in the double size bed and to try to get as comfy as the flock mattress and the coats used in place of blankets would allow. This night, however, before any of their feet touched the bottom step of the narrow staircase PC Shaw returned to the house. He just appeared in the middle room as if out of thin air. In fact, straight out of the bloody blue like an unexpected shot in the dark. 'The front door must have been open and the cheeky bugger must've walked right though the house 'cause there he stood as large as bloody life', Bill reasoned. The

Policeman's face, often flushed with the embarrassment of a novice in training, drained of colour before Bill's very eyes as with the most serious of tones he solemnly said:

"Could I have a word, Mr Hackney? There seems to be a few discrepancies emerging surrounding Kenneth's whereabouts. I don't think I've been on a hiding for nothing after all."

'What were discrepancies' Wilf wondered as he strained to listen and overhear what was being said but the only thing he heard was the sound of the door closing as his Father and the policeman went into the parlour together. What little respite Wilf had known instantly dissipated faster than the morning dew on the playing fields as Fear immediately returned to grip his heart with even more gusto than She had before. He managed however, in spite of Her suffocating presence, to place one of his almost twelve yet going on twenty-one-year old arms around Alma and the other one around Billy as he gently pulled them closer to him as they huddled together poised at the bottom of the stairs.

In spite of his best efforts Wilf had not managed to make any sense of the muffled voices at all but felt as if cold water was running straight down the middle of his back. 'Perhaps Kenneth had been hurt and couldn't be moved. Perhaps if he had been injured a doctor had been sent for. Someone might even have taken him to Westcliffe hospital cum institution cum former bloody workhouse' thoughts tumbled around in his young mind. They never went near the burial grounds of the old workhouse when they were playing close to the institution. It was a spooky place and he hoped to God that Kenneth wasn't up there. Whatever had happened, something was definitely wrong. He hadn't needed to hear it to believe it because every hair on the back of his neck responded to it. He forced his legs that were feeling as heavy as tree trunks to move as he led Alma and Billy up the narrow steep stairs and into the back bedroom. It was strange to be going to bed without his brother. It simply left too much space in the bed as they snuggled one at the top, instead of two, and two at the bottom as usual. Wilf immediately missed his confidant and became acutely aware that he would have nobody to share his secrets and dreams with when the other two had fallen asleep. Only the night before after Alma and Billy had dropped off to sleep Wilf shared his hopes and ambitions for the future with his brother and closest friend. 'Perhaps they would go into business together. They could start a homemade sweet shop and fill it with things like black treacle toffee and coconut ice, another one of Wilf's delicacies'. Wilf could also manage scones and macaroons at a push but then that would have made it a cake shop and, given the choice, they would both rather own a sweetie shop any day. It was also decided, at one of their hushed parleys, that they would certainly travel the country or even the world together if only to watch their delicacies be taken with tea across the four corners of the globe. They were determined to set their sights high simply because if they aimed for nothing then they would surely hit it every time.

The repercussions of war fuelled adult dreams and filled hearts with a desperate hunger for love, life and liberty and children were captivated and caught up in the ricochet of it all. Kenneth loved to draw and had the ability to make a good job of it. His forte was birds. He could draw starlings, sparrows and robins and Miss Jardine the schoolmistress, had even taken one of his drawings home with her to put up on her kitchen wall. 'So perhaps one day someone would buy one of his pictures and between them, because they always did everything together, they'd make a small fortune and become rich. What fun, they'd have' they schemed and plotted together. If they made enough money they would never be cold in the middle of winter again and they would have hot water at the turn of a tap whenever they wanted it. A wardrobe of new clothes, not second or third hand ones, and even, because the sky would be the limit, a cashmere coat and a pair of the finest leather shoes. They would own clean and proper bedding including sheets and pillows, a nightshirt to wear and even a pot of their own to piss in. They tried to stifle their laughter by pushing corners of the overcoat into their mouths as they took turns at trying to speak in a posh voice. In the end, Wilf's political reasoning sobered their fun and put an end to their conversation and laughter as he adopted a broad and exaggerated intonation:

"They can tack us as they bloody find us or not at all! We're as good as the next bugger and ten times better than some. We're all born equal in this world and we mack our own luck and good fortune. We'll play the hand that's been dealt us, our Ken, as best we can. No bugger's insignificant. No bugger, including us. We all have a part to play in life. I've said it before and I'll say it again, they can tack us as they find us and if they dunna bloody like us then they'll have to bloody lump us and it'll be their loss not ours!"

Wilf was not allowed to swear in front of adults especially his parents who told him time and time again, in no uncertain terms, to 'do as I bloody say and not as I bloody do'. Translated this simply meant that it was perfectly acceptable for adults to swear and curse as much and as often as they liked but not for children to get away with it. Any child who uttered so much as a 'bloody' or a 'bugger' had their mouths washed out with the foulest of soaps. Women and girls created a disgusting slimy detergent from any soap-like leftovers by stuffing all the bits and pieces of anything that resembled soap into an old tin can. Over time the concoction fermented into something slimy and horrible that was commonly known as 'soft soap'. It was wise advice therefore for a child to keep their lips tightly buttoned whenever they thought a swear word might slip through them because the taste of soft soap lingered for bloody months! Whenever Wilf was left in charge however he thought he 'ruled the roost' and when he was sure that he was out of earshot of his parents, or anyone else who might cant on him, he felt it an integral part of his role to say 'bloody' and 'bugger' as much and as often as he fancied. In fact, he thought it underlined his authority and superiority and went hand-in-hand with the immense burden of responsibility that had been placed across the back of his puerile shoulders.

Recollections of Kenneth made Wilf feel sombre as he started to realise, although embryonic, the intensity of longing, loneliness and agony that occurs after a person loses something or someone they desperately wanted to keep. He was quickly jolted back into time and reality as he overheard the voice of his Father: "I'll get 'em back up, Nell. We'll have to get someone to watch 'em for us tonight" before he opened the door to the bottom of the stairs and called up to his bairns:

"Wilf, get 'em all up and get your backsides down here as fast as you bloody can. We've all got work to do tonight". Wilf, followed by Alma and Billy rushed out of bed and back down the stairs two at a time. Wilf thought his legs, that had turned to jelly as opposed to feeling like tree trunks, would give way beneath him at any second. He could not comprehend what was happening. He was light headed and felt funny inside. He thought he was standing still because he was sure his feet weren't moving and yet the room was spinning round. He tried to stabilise his sensations by fixing his gaze on familiar objects in the room. His Mother had just finished feeding Terrence and was about to put him in the sheet-lined bottom drawer that served both as his cot and his cradle. The only good thing, as far as Wilf could tell, was that PC Shaw was nowhere in the house and would not therefore be questioning him about his brother.

Within seconds Bill left the room to answer a muffled knock on the front door and Wilf detected the suppressed and hushed tones of a man's voice swiftly followed by the sound of the door being firmly closed. 'Oh God, please don't let it be the policeman. I dunna want to be taken to the station an' be arrested an' be locked away in the dark' Wilf's thoughts raced as his legs wobbled and his knees knocked for all they were worth.

"It was Archie Williams from the end of the road", Bill said as he turned to Nell with his chin almost on his chest. "They've heard about our Kenneth and wanted to know if they could do anything to help us out. They've offered to take the children for the night. Put 'em up for us. I said we'd be grateful for it. That's right Nell isn't it? We are grateful for it, aren't we?"

Nell nodded but said nothing in acknowledgement of his statement as she buttoned, unbuttoned and re-buttoned her blouse after feeding her youngest bairn. 'He'll last 'til the morning now' she thought and it was just as well that he would.

Bill looked at his three bairns as they stood huddled together by the open door at the bottom of the stairs and shook his head in disbelief. Farming out his kids would never have entered his head in a month of Sundays. What an unbelievable and unthinkable situation beset them. If any man had told him that this would have happened at the start of the day then he would have called him a bloody liar. Now here he was, all six foot two of him, submitting to the cold-hearted demands of Fate as he relinquished his brood, minus his blonde haired 'un, to Archie Williams and his wife. He hoped beyond hope that this would in some way shield his bairns from what looked like bein' a very long night and that their kindness would somehow shelter them from the storm that was brewin'.

Wilf was too afraid to ask why they were being 'put up' across the road, but suddenly, from somewhere deep inside, he discovered a glimmer of courage that enabled him momentarily to overcome his partial paralysis. In an almost inaudible voice and with trembling legs and heart he longingly asked "Is Kenneth all right Dad? Have they found him yet? Is he all right?"

"No. They haven't found him yet, Son. He'll be fine though, don't ya worry yoursen. He's a survivor that lad. He'll be fine" his Father replied with as much confidence as he could scrape together. He spoke out his thoughts with hope in his voice in an attempt to convince himself more than anyone else that his Son, his beautiful Son, would soon be discovered safe and well.

"You all get a good night's sleep with Mr and Mrs Williams. It's getting on for nine and it's way past your bedtime. Behave yourselves and remember to use your manners at the Williams's. I don't want 'em talkin' about us an' sayin' you've all been bloody dragged up. Remember your manners" Nell repeated like a parrot. In a complete state of flux they prepared to leave the house. Bill picked up Terrence en bloc in the bottom drawer that cradled him and held it like a huge treasure chest of immense value safely and securely in his strong arms. Nell stood like a sentry by the front door and as each one of her children passed her she said

"Good night and God bless" to each one of them in turn. Yet Nell sensed that it might not be a good night and if God was in His heaven then they would certainly need His blessing. Nell was of the persuasion that there would be 'no peace for the wicked in this world' and because she did not class herself nor any of her own as wicked then her lad would be returned to them safe and well. After all, she believed that 'you only reap what you sow in life and none of them had sown a wild oat between 'em and would never do any bugger a bad turn if they could do 'em a good 'en'. Therefore she trusted that all would be well. It had to be because she believed that the scales of truth and justice were always well balanced and fair.

Bill holding the drawer containing Terrence firmly across his broad chest led his entire family, apart from his blonde curly haired 'un, down to the bottom of the street. Every one of them played out their individual part with precision as if the best of actors in a scene from a melancholy play. Curtains moved slightly on every side of the road, veiled eyes watched and tongues, as sure as night followed day, would undoubtedly wag. The children followed Bill's example and fixed their faces looking straight ahead as they walked, almost in procession, across and down the road to their ultimate and most unlikely of destinations. Although it was only a short walk to the house at the end of their street it felt as if they were moving a million miles away from the security of their roughshod yet familiar surroundings. Not one of the entourage looked back.

Bill did not return home after he left his children with the couple who would prove to be the truest of neighbours in an hour of desperate need but took up the search for his boy again. 'He must be somewhere. He couldn't have vanished into thin air. Now could he?' he reasoned.

Archie and his wife Elsie did not have any children of their own. They were quiet, reserved and softly spoken people. Their house stood out not just because it was the biggest one but because it was also considered by many to be the best and the cleanest one too. The step and windowsills were regularly red-leaded and as a result of vinegar, water and copious amounts of elbow grease the door and windows gleamed in the summer sunshine. Nell took her hat off to Elsie for her diligence and regularly stated that the external impression of a house demanded eminence in a woman's cleaning regime purely because 'you had more passers-by your house than you ever had callers-in'.

In spite of the fact that only two people lived in the house, Archie and Elsie had their own corrugated Anderson shelter half buried in soil at the bottom of their small back garden. Such extravagance, coupled with perceived affluence, fuelled the opinion that Archie and Elsie Williams thought themselves to be 'a cut above the rest' of the inhabitants of the street and too bloody good to rub shoulders with any of their neighbours. Some even thought them 'penny wise and pound foolish' when it came to money matters having accumulated so many possessions including their own bloody Anderson shelter.

Other neighbours simply thought that Mr Williams had looked after his pennies and his pounds had obviously looked after themselves. It was a very strange turn of events indeed that resulted in Nell's children being cared for in this house out of all the other houses in the street. Nell however always tried to give people the benefit of the doubt in all situations. She reasoned that 'you should never judge a book by its cover' and however foolish and lavish generosity appeared it was always better than being tighter than a duck's arse! So she kept her opinions to herself unless asked for and tried never to judge a person unless she'd walked a mile in their shoes.

As Wilf stepped over the threshold of the house just a stone's throw away from his own he entered another world and, in different circumstances, he would have soaked up every minute of it including the pampering. The rooms in the house were decked out with the finest furniture he had ever set eyes on; not that he'd seen very much furniture in his eleven years. The quality and décor was such that it made the three of them feel immediately uncomfortable in fact so uncomfortable that they didn't dare move a muscle or blink an eyelid. Mrs Williams made some strong tea. They weren't used to strong tea but it had a spoon of real sugar in it so tasted delicious. They ate, as delicately as they possibly could, a supper of dropped scones and homemade jam in virtual silence. They had been told often enough that children should be seen and not heard and had therefore been so afraid of saying something wrong that they all united in saying nothing at all. The silence lasted until Mrs Williams decided to break the ice by putting a record on the gramophone to entertain them. 'What a treat! A real gramophone and record; what an absolute treat!' Wilf instinctively turned to look at the expression of delight painted across Kenneth's face but just as quickly realised that he was not there with them. He had not shared their feast of tea and scones prompting Wilf to wonder if his brother, wherever he was, felt hungry but the voice of Vera Lynn distracted him as the gramophone crackled out the familiar words of hope:

We'll meet again
Don't know where,
Don't know when
But I know we'll meet again some sunny day.
Keep smiling through,
Just like you always do
Till the blue skies drive the dark clouds far away.

But Wilf hadn't felt like smiling. In fact, he thought he would never smile again until Kenneth returned safe and sound and then the pair of them, the blonde curly haired 'un and the Italian looking lad, would laugh their bloody socks off; always assuming, of course, that they were fortunate enough to have a pair of socks on their feet in the first place.

Sometimes, what goes round comes round in life and on that long and dark July night in 1941 kindness, although uncomfortable to accept, was shown to Wilf, Alma, Billy, and baby Terrence. Years later Alma would return, many times over, the generosity shown to them and, by a quirk of events or by divine instigation some of the furniture in the house would form part of her own personal possessions. As for Wilf, he would have preferred to forget the events of the night altogether and wipe them off the slate of his memory forever. If he could he would have locked the events of the day in Davy Jones's locker and thrown away the key but Vera Lynn and the words of the song: 'We'll meet again' would never, ever allow him to do that.

Used to having one bed, no pillows and certainly no blankets, especially during the summer time, all the children found it difficult to get off to sleep but all for very different reasons. Alma lay on her own in a beautiful bed, complete with pillow and even a clean pure cotton pillowcase. Whilst she felt like a princess, in no uncertain terms, she missed the security afforded her by the presence of her three brothers. Wilf and Billy were put up together in a big double bed that had a solid wooden headboard, real blankets, and even a handmade patchwork quilt resting on top of it. Four year-old Billy missed Alma's arm around his shoulder and the safety of his brothers' legs and feet either side his body so, in a voice barely recognisable, he whispered, "Please can I sleep at the bottom of the bed, our Wilf? I conna get to sleep at the top end. It doesn't feel right".

"Course ya can our Bill" Wilf whispered. "Be as quiet as a mouse though. We dunna want Mrs Williams comin' back up to see us again. Hers got her hands full with our Terrence and besides she's already tucked us up twice and made us say our bedtime prayers so I dunna want be tucked up again and have to go all through that rigmarole. So, go on, move now and be quick and quiet about it."

With this Billy shuffled as silently as he could around the edge of the bed until he reached its footboard and eventually went to sleep in his familiar and safe head to toe position. Had Wilf been in the King of England's bed he would still not have managed a wink of sleep. He felt very uncomfortable indeed as he contemplated the trauma of the day. He went over and over the day's events in his troubled mind. He relived time and again the last time he had seen his brother Kenneth. Had he been at home underneath the overcoat that doubled up as a blanket, lying on the uneven flock mattress then he would surely have 'spilled the beans' and blurted out the truth. But he hadn't been at home and he couldn't tell anyone the truth of the matter. He couldn't relieve his conscience and set the record straight. It was far too late for that now. Where would he start his story and who would believe him? he questioned himself. The condemning accusations and echoes of Guilt filled his head and his thoughts would not rest long enough to allow him to fall asleep to the soothing sounds of 'We'll Meet Again'. In the most bizarre surroundings, he silently wrestled alone in the deepest darkness of night with the invisible puppet masters of Fear and Guilt. He had never imagined that he would long for a cramped flock bed filled with feet, legs, arms and hands; but he did. In an attempt to comfort himself he thought about the wonderful plans he had made with Kenneth for their future lives together and convinced himself, in the face of condemnation, that Kenneth would be back home tomorrow and he'd enjoy telling him about the gramophone, the tea and scones and the bed that was fit for Winston Churchill himself to sleep in.

CHAPTER SIX – A BURIAL

The sun broke through a small tear in the tightly closed blackout curtains. Amazingly, its rays illuminated a hand-tied posy of limp buttercups and daisies that had been gently placed in the middle of the small coffin laid to rest on top of the Morrison shelter in the front room. By removing its welded wire mesh sides the shelter could double-up and be used as a 6' 6" (2m) x 4' 0" (1.2m) x 2' 6" (0.75m) high table. As part of the Government's free distribution of the shelters Bill received and assembled its three hundred and odd parts by using the three tools provided to make the job easier. Nowhere in the instructions however had it mentioned that the shelter could be used as a coffin bier.

Nell sat butt up to the coffin and was as close as she could possibly get to it. She rested her hand alongside the posy she had picked off the top of the Hill earlier that morning and sat gently tap tapping the coffin lid as if to soothe and comfort the small body inside. She was miles away, thinking of the times she had nursed her lad better, after making poultices of goose oil and camphor to ease

63

his chesty coughs that often threatened to develop into the worst kind of croup imaginable. She had recently allowed him to be immunised against diphtheria setting an example, as the unofficial midwife, to all the mothers in the village. She had taken him, held him, forced him to have the injection to protect him from the deadly infection but there was no vaccination against death, especially a death of this kind. Although she longed to reach in through the hard shell that encased her son and hold her lad close to her heart just one more time, she dared not even lift the lid. Bill had identified Kenneth's body late on Saturday night and firmly told her to 'let him lie, leave him be. Best to remember him as he was' and mercifully she had not looked at the body of her boy. Nell had laid out and prepared more dead bodies, including stillborn bairns, than she cared to remember but, if she was truthful, she would have to admit that she was relieved to obey Bill's command and entrust the care of her lad, for his final journey, to someone else. Her pain was exacerbated by the fact that they did not have enough money to buy a shroud to clothe his small, once beautiful, body in. They had not planned for a funeral especially for one of their little 'uns. They had no insurance and had been forced to fall on the mercy of the local undertaker who promised Nell that her lovely blonde haired lad would not be buried naked. She trusted in his promise because there was nothing else for it. She could not have borne the thought of her boy lying cold and bare inside a coffin they would be paying for in small instalments for many months to come. Grief filled her heart and her home engulfing them all with a deep and heavy darkness that was almost physical in presence. Although the room was full with people no one spoke in an audible voice. Only whispers in the darkness could occasionally be heard accompanied by muffled sniffles and tentative tears. Men passed Woodbine cigarettes around the room whilst the women, holding the tiniest of sherry glasses, sipped what was left from the Christmas bottle of Halls Wine as if it was the very best of French cognac.

Nell felt completely exhausted and yet somehow managed to retain an air of composure and dignity. The events of the past five days including the sham of an inquest conducted only the day before remained fresh in her mind. At the same time, however, nothing seemed real as overwhelming shock and numbness procured an air of utter disbelief and total abandonment. As Nell embraced the last few moments alongside the coffin of her beautiful boy a minute fraction of the immense reality of her loss threatened to overwhelm and suffocate her. Suddenly, she struggled to catch her breath as Grief started to crush the remaining fragments of life from the depths of her broken heart. In that instant of momentary truth she realised that saying goodbye to her lad would generate more pain than she could possibly endure. It was then, in that very moment of acute awareness, that deep within her she felt the turn of an invisible switch as she determined to give Grief a run for His money. She would show Him that He could not dampen nor dent her dignity and in so doing destroy her spirit. Consciously now, her wits amazingly about her, she scanned the bigger picture.

'The country was at war. The world was at war' she reasoned. 'Mothers' sons were being maimed and killed every day of the bloody week. Too many boys belonging to too many Mothers would never be coming home' she reasoned. 'Weren't tragedy and death integral parts and parcels of life and living anyway?' she internally questioned, oblivious to everything and everyone else in the room. 'Courage, duty and dignity were paramount to the defence and morale of the nation' she continued her interrogation. And so, with her hand still caressing the small wooden coffin Nell determined that she would not shed another tear. 'Tears were signs of weakness anyway'; and, 'what's more' she concluded, 'she would not allow any of her kith and kin to cry either. She'd make sure of it. Yes, as sure as night follows day, she'd make damn sure of it'. Somewhere within the depths of her being and at the centre of the worst pain imaginable, a switch of self-preservation had been turned on and would prove to have lasting repercussions.

At that very moment of unstinting resolve and as if in the nick of time Nell heard the most solemn, awful words echo round the small overcrowded room. The words were so terrible that the four walls, that had already concealed so many secrets, were unable to absorb and simply deflected them straight back into the room:

"It's time, Mrs Hackney. I'm sorry, but it's time. We need to be on our way", declared the chief undertaker perfectly balancing compassion and efficiency as he stepped forward to take control of the formalities of the situation.

Nell looked around the full, yet empty, room for the eyes of Bill. He was standing upright next to the front door as the bearers, clutching strong ropes between their calloused hands, swooped as one over Kenneth's coffin momentarily blocking out the chamfer of sunlight that had dared to break through the darkness.

Nell wanted to scream at the top of her voice: 'Don't touch him. Don't you dare touch him! Don't take my boy. Leave my lad be.'

But if she had started to scream then she would never have stopped and surely the mouths of the neighbours had already been stuffed with enough gossip to last 'em all a bloody lifetime an a half. She would not be providing them with anything more to discuss over their backyard walls. So Nell swallowed her pain, a pill that tasted as bitter as the most rancid of butters. But, if she thought she could silence Grief so easily, she was very mistaken as she heard Him sternly say through her very own lips:

"Head up, shoulders back, an' if any bugger cries I'll give 'em somehat to cry for when we get back". "No tears, you hear me, no bloody tears".

An almighty gasp filled the room as Nell raised herself up as straight as a die whilst putting her shoulders rigidly back and lifting her head proudly into the air. She would be the first of her brood to set an example and woe-betide any of 'em that didn't follow her lead.

Wilf was ready in a fashion having been up since the crack of dawn cleaning shoes and helping to get the Sunday best clothes ready. He had also been put in charge of providing everyone with a black satin armband which Nell had made the day before. Nell's family had been sent for from Nelson in Lancashire and the saying 'that many hands make light work' had proved true in the saddest of situations. Wilf's cousin Dorothy had helped him to dress Alma and Billy who were both having a hard time trying to understand why Kenneth was dead and what dead really meant. Nobody knew how to explain to any of the children what had happened to their brother. Alma had grasped only titbits of hushed conversations since Sunday morning when Mr Williams had told them that they would not be seeing their brother again because he'd gone to be with God in heaven. She had enough common sense therefore to comprehend, in a childlike way, that the family were getting ready for their brother's funeral. She would not however be able to believe that they would soon be carrying him to be buried in the churchyard on the Hill and she would never see him again.

Wilf, on the other hand, knew only too well that he had lost his younger brother, his confidant and his friend and what's more he blamed himself entirely and solely for his loss. Everything had happened so quickly. Who would have believed on Saturday, that fateful day, five days ago, that Kenneth would breathe his last in this war-torn world? 'If only he had known what the end result of the day was going to be then he would have tried to rob Fate and Death of their young prey. He would have bartered with them both in an attempt to change places with his brother whom he loved more than life itself.' Dying, in comparison to the huge burden Wilf was to carry for the rest of his life, would have been a generous exchange. His morose thoughts were pervaded as he watched his Mother with the tightest of lips turn her back on his brother's coffin. He could have spared her, his Father, his Brothers and Sister, his entire family this anguish and heartache if only, oh if only, he had known. Guilt had a secret, yet firm, hold of Wilf's heart and mind and He was never going to let him go free.

Nell quickly eyed her three bairns. She did not know how it had happened but her children were all dressed in their Sunday best clothes and all wore black armbands. Terrence was wrapped in a shawl and was being held by her sister Florrie who had pinned a black satin ribbon to one of his bootees in recognition of the loss of a brother he would never know. Nell swiftly yanked Wilf's cap off the top of his head and threw it onto the floor as she sternly reinforced her command:

"No tears. Did you hear me Wilf? No bloody tears, unless you want something to cry for when we get back."

The bearers firmly wrapped the ropes around the top and the underneath of Kenneth's coffin. Everyone stood back, completely engulfed and totally helpless. It was possible to have heard a pin drop into the silence of the room.

Someone opened the front door wide putting strain on the hinges that held it in place. The sunlight flooded the room penetrating and illuminating the sorrowful scene as if trespassing on the very ground where Death, Despair and Darkness reigned.

Four burly bearers led the small procession outside and into the stillness of the street that was bathed in the rays and warmth of July sunshine. The experienced undertakers knew just how much rope was needed to secure and carry the coffin without it touching the floor. Bill and Nell, standing as straight as they possibly could, took their positions behind the coffin in the middle of road. Wilf, Alma and Billy stood in a straight line behind their parents. Wilf took centre position with Alma and Billy either side of him. Relatives, including Florrie who held Terrence tightly in her arms, fell in line behind the rest of the family. They painted as sad a picture as had ever been seen in the village on the Hill. Obeying Nell's command and following their parents' example, they all raised their rounded shoulders, lifted their heads to face the sun and, in so doing, created formidable long dark shadows on the cobbled road behind them.

It was just three streets walk to the small Methodist chapel up John Street, into Church Street and finally down the High Street. Nell kept her gaze firmly fixed straight ahead as if in some kind of morbid trance. She had been so stunned by the whole event that she did not notice her posy of buttercups and daisies fall to the ground and be trampled underfoot by the increasing number of friends and neighbours who merged with the cortège en route to the chapel. Strangely though, Nell did notice that all the curtains, upstairs and down, in every house along every street were tightly closed as if in obedience to a curfew; not a pair had been left open. 'A sign of sincere respect' Nell thought. Doors silently opened and closed as an army of mourners joined the procession on its way to the chapel falling in line behind the grief-stricken family.

Just as they turned into the top of Church Street, Sam Squires a mellow tenor in the church choir and one of the men who had helped lead the search for Kenneth started to softly sing:

There's a Friend for little children,
Above the bright, blue sky,
A Friend who never changes,
Whose love will never die.

Quite unexpectedly, it felt as if the street filled with angels and that their voices merged as one with the choir of rough-looking, common men whose emotions overflowed into their voices. 'Had Angels, messengers from God, been sent to earth to help and strengthen them in their distress?' Nell thought. Bill had told her on more than one occasion, his version of the story of the battle of Mons in Belgium, where on 23 August 1914 British troops saw angels throw a protective curtain around them to save them from disaster.' Nell however refused to believe in anything anymore and quickly dismissed the thought of angels as she walked rigidly behind the coffin of her boy. 'If there was a force for good, if there was a God in Heaven, then how and why could this be happening to them? What had they or their nine-year-old bairn ever done to deserve this?' she questioned the elements.

The world seemed to be running in slow motion; as if watching a black and white film when the reel had started to slow down and nothing made much sense as words and pictures merged into each other. In spite of this Nell did not shed a tear and one look, over her shoulder, at her bairns, ensured that they firmly locked them away too. They would not become the focus of any bugger's pity especially today.

Wilf did not want to believe that his brother was inside the wooden box, the coffin that swung gently along the very streets where they had laughed and played together so many times. He could hear the words "there's a home for little children above the bright blue sky" as it was being sung in the most reverent of tones but found it difficult to understand its meaning. Although the July sunshine undoubtedly did light up the sky it wasn't bright blue to him. It felt as grey and as heavy as the thickest of blankets. In fact, he thought the sky would never look blue again. His life would soon fast forward. Before he knew what had hit him he would be fourteen and his Father would probably find him a job alongside him at the local steelworks and his hopes, aspirations and dreams would all hit the floor. He would never raid apples again and yet that wouldn't matter too much now he reasoned, because he would have no brother to raid the orchard with anymore. In fact, he'd have no brother to do anything with anymore. There was too much of an age gap between himself and his younger brother Bill for them ever to become pals and playmates. Anyway, nobody could ever take his Kenneth's place or come close to ever filling his shoes and the thought of it made him want to cry his heart out. At that very moment, his breaking point, Nell looked over her shoulder again to silently but sternly reinforce her command. The thought of her words reverberated through every bone in his almost adolescent body, taking possession of his young heart and mind: 'No tears, you hear me, no bloody tears else I'll give ya somehat to cry for when we get back'.

Wilf felt unable to contain his feelings any longer. He thought he was about to cry his eyes out and the tears would burst through every pore in his young body. He bit down hard on the inside of his cheek until the taste of blood filled his mouth. He would not cry, he dare not cry. He would not surrender to the tears not solely because he was petrified of his Mother's retribution, although that was paramount in his mind, but because he also feared the effects his tears might have on his brother and sister walking either side him. He had to set them the right example by obeying his Mother's command. He was too afraid and too obedient to cry even though he wanted to unlock the floodgates and openly weep for the brother who lay in the coffin ahead of him with or without a shroud on his back.

Nell sincerely believed that she had taught her brood a hard lesson that day, a lesson that would equip them to face whatever the rest of life threw at them. After all, she contemplated 'there were no guarantees and no free passes given out in life. Yes she'd teach 'em the hard way that there wasn't any room in life for tears, no place for wallowing in self-pity, not in the real world. They didn't live in a bloody fairytale with a 'happy ever after' Walt Disney ending. This was life and they'd best get used to it. Her job was to put a thick skin on their backs and by God she'd do it and one day they'd understand her reasoning and thank her for it. Yes, surely they would' she tried to convince herself as if to exorcise the last half ounce of Guilt that lingered lodged in the corner of heart.

They reached the main road and as they turned the corner the small Wesleyan chapel came into view. As if in an instant they reached the first base of Kenneth's final journey. The procession stopped abruptly. The bearers lifted the lad shoulder high as they prepared to scale the twelve steps up to the huge wooden chapel doors. Nell could see the young Methodist minister waiting for them at the top. He had tried his best to console her, to comfort her but Nell was way past the bounds of consolation and in no mood for Holy Joes. She had faithfully had all four of her bairns christened at a Methodist chapel and apart from Wilf, who had been baptised at the Abbey, they had been 'done' at this very one. She had religiously sent all three, including Kenneth, off to Sunday school morning and afternoon since they were knee-high and old enough to walk and talk. 'What bloody good had it done?' she questioned herself and 'Where was God when her lad had needed him?' In the midst of this dark valley of the shadow of Death Nell could not sense any glimmer of life, light nor hope. It was pitch dark in the depths of her soul. Every motion, every breath, was perfunctory, and, if there truly was a friend for little children above the bright bloody blue sky, then she was grateful to Him for the anaesthetic. She felt nothing, nothing at all.

"I am the resurrection and the life. He who believes in me, though he were dead yet shall he live." were the words Nell heard as she walked, stiff as a board, down the left hand aisle behind the coffin of her blonde curly haired boy. The family sat on the front pews in the centre section whilst the mourners filed in behind them overflowing into the right and left hand sides of the chapel. Some friends and neighbours scaled the stairs to the balcony choir stalls to peer down on the solemn scene. Each pew was separated from the next and had a small wooden door on either side of the aisles. Every door had its own latch which the undertakers swiftly turned immediately the pew was full as if to lock the mourners inside it. "Click, click, click" the locks went as the chapel filled to capacity. The undertakers need not however have taken the time or the trouble to turn the locks. There was no escape and nowhere to run or hide from what was happening.

As soon as Kenneth was positioned at the front of the chapel the Minister nodded to the organist who looked over the top of his glasses before starting to pipe out a loud chord of music. The regiment of mourners stood, took up a hymnal and started to softly sing

"All things bright and beautiful
All creatures' great and small
All things wise and wonderful
The Lord God made them all".

Nell stared at the table upon which her son's coffin rested. It had the words 'The Lamb of God' engraved across the front of it. She focused on them and wondered what on earth they could possibly mean before noticing that her posy of buttercups and daisies was nowhere to be seen on the coffin of her boy. It looked bare and lifeless, a reflection of her heart, bereft and in a state of coma.

The rest of the day, including the finality of the committal, was nothing but a blur in Wilf's mind. He remembered the ropes tied firmly around the wrists of the bearers as they carried his brother from the chapel down the High Street to the Church of England churchyard but mercifully little else. What was to be etched on his mind forever was what happened when the family got back home after the funeral was over.

Wilf, like the rest of his family, in one way or another, returned to an empty house without his brother and his closest friend. Florrie put Terrence, who had slept for most of the day, in the bottom drawer of the tallboy while Dorothy went into the kitchen to put the kettle onto the stove. Nell rolled up her sleeves and physically lined up her trio of bairns in the middle room. Bill, oblivious to what Nell was about to do, was totally taken aback by what transpired. Wilf stood at the head of the small line as if standing to attention and, without thinking instinctively left a space for Kenneth, as usual, next to him. Nell, with a face like thunder, firmly pushed him along to close the gap until there was no space between him and his sister Alma. At once there was a noticeable difference in the height of the two children giving the impression that Nell had gone many years without having had a bairn between the two of them.

'Was this how the space, the huge gap, the gaping hole left by Kenneth was to be filled? By pushing him along until he occupied not only his own place in the family circle but Kenneth's as well. Almost as if his brother had never been born' Wilf silently thought. Alma found herself standing next to Wilf instead of Kenneth and with a vice-like grip she grasped Billy's hand; afraid to let him go in case something awful happened to him. In case he died too. Nell stood directly in front of them and like the sternest of schoolmarms, she quite calmly declared: "Kenneth's dead and that's the end of him. No one is to ever mention his name again. Do you hear me? No one." Just in case they had not heard or misunderstood what she had said, she reiterated her order: "Kenneth's dead and that's the end of him. No one is to ever mention his name again. Do you hear me? No one."

In an expression of the most intense grief and pain imaginable, she had hammered in her son's coffin nails, firmly fastening the lid down. It would never, in any way shape or form, be opened again. She continued her statement of literal logic. "There's nothing down the churchyard. Kenneth's not there and thait be down there soon enough. There's plenty a people down there that'd swap places with you so no bugger will be visiting his grave. Do ya hear me, no bugger, never, ever?"

Wilf was unable to digest his Mother's words. They were confusing, a contradiction of terms. 'If Kenneth wasn't down the churchyard then how could anyone be down there with him soon enough and how could people down the cemetery want to swap places with him?' He thought his head would burst as blood pulsated through his temples.

Having said her piece Nell started to dust, clean and prepare a Spam tea in a frightful frenzied state. Bill went into the front room to busy himself refitting the mesh sides to the Morrison shelter in anticipation of a night of air raids. 'Life had to go on. It could not stop because they had lost their boy. As tragic as it was, life had to go on. The country was at war' became the ethos behind their actions.

Wilf wanted to run a mile, disappear. He wanted to escape the reality of the fact that no matter how much you loved and sacrificed, no matter how hard you worked and how much treacle toffee you made, it did not guarantee that you would not make a mistake, just one mistake, and lose the most important and precious thing in your life, a part of your family and a huge part of your heart. On 9th July 1941 Wilf promised himself that he would never again be responsible for losing someone he loved and neither would he give away something he desperately wanted to keep. He sensed that the impact and effects of loss directly equated to how much a person wanted to keep that which was lost to them. Wilf had wanted to keep his brother more than life itself. He would have gladly stood in his brother's stead and given his own life in exchange for his. Not only had he lost his second in command but a brother for whom he had been responsible. Never again would Kenneth laugh at jokes and play Knock and Run at the doors down the street where they lived. He would never have the opportunity to become the artist he dared to dream of being. The two of them would never open a sweetie shop and travel the world together. His brother would never grow up and know the joy of becoming a father and raising a family of his own. At almost twelve, but going on twenty-one, Wilf started to learn that loss was like a merciless monster that could extract the very lifeblood from a living heart and life. What he did not know, however, what he could not have possibly known, was that Grief's suppressed power was only an embryo within his young heart; the heart of a boy whose mouth had filled with blood as he denied his tears and buried them as deep as they had buried his brother; six foot under.

The next morning, in the very early hours, while the house was still asleep trying to absorb the repercussions of the previous day, Nell quietly washed herself and baby Terrence before stuffing a small bag with clothes. She fed and wrapped her bairn in his one and only shawl and tore the mourning ribbon off his bootee before throwing the black satin band into the fire. She watched the flames consume it until there was not a single thread of it left. In a cool as a cucumber mood she poured out a second cup of tea for herself.

Wilf had been unable to sleep. Although there was more room to stretch out in the double bed it was too big for three of them. It felt so empty; there was just too much room to spare. Wilf started to realise that nothing would ever fill the space that Kenneth had left behind as he tossed and turned the night away. He relived the events of recent days over and over in his troubled mind but always ended up hitting a brick wall as he tried to recount the blur of the funeral and burial. His thoughts in the morning light were overtaken by muffled voices of his relatives from Lancashire as they moved around downstairs and spoke quietly together underneath him in the middle room. He had heard his Father leave the house at the crack of dawn and go down the yard and out through the back gate to turn up for work and duty as usual. Life was going on as normal. His Mother said that it must and it would. They could not afford the privilege of a respectable mourning period.

Wilf heard the distinctive sound of the front door as it opened and closed quietly. The house fell strangely silent. He strained to hear the familiar sounds of his Mother as she busied herself making breakfast whilst, at the same time, cradling and feeding Terrence but all he heard was the sound of footsteps, almost in unison, walking down the cobbled street outside. Not wanting to disturb Alma or Billy he very carefully sidled out of bed, his heart pounding. Something was wrong. He walked through into his parents' bedroom and peeked out through the centre join of the blackout curtains. He blinked and rubbed his eyes to make sure he wasn't seeing things. He stared at them long and hard and enough to bore holes straight through the middle of their backs. He watched intently until all three of them disappeared around the corner at the top of the street. Florrie and Dorothy were each carrying a bag and flanked his Mother who was walking in-between them holding baby Terrence. They walked woefully yet determinedly down the street and not one of them ever looked back before turning the corner and disappearing from sight. They had left before the streets started to wake up and without saying goodbye to any of the children. Wilf closed the curtains to keep out the light as he slumped down on the floor in the corner of the small sad bedroom and whispered: "It's all my fault. All this is my fault". He would have wept without restraint and fear of reprisal into the safety of the lonely darkness had his pain and his tears not have been buried with his brother in the cemetery on the Hill.

CHAPTER SEVEN –

A WEDDING AND A CAKE

Because Brenda was expecting a baby, Wilf married her on 16 December 1950. In such a precarious situation, marriage was deemed the only honourable solution to such a shameful state of affairs. In fact, in such dire circumstances, there was no other option and nothing else for it. Having been backed into a corner, the only way out was to 'face the music and marry' or risk dying of gunshot wounds for trying to escape and shirk responsibility. That much said, Wilf did in fact love Brenda with all his heart and determined to marry her from the first moment he saw her. Alma, his sister, had smuggled secret love letters to and fro between the two of them for almost a year. Notes in which Wilf regularly asked Brenda to meet him in one of their secret locations. It was all purely platonic, of course! On one memorable occasion however they met outside the local picture palace. Wilf paid for them both to go in, a sure sign of commitment, to see the latest film 'The Toast of New Orleans' (MGM 1950) starring Mario Lanza, a famous tenor of his time and generation. Wilf was half-expecting Brenda, as she had done before, to bring along a few sweets of some description and was more than a little surprised when she appeared with a bag full of actual lemons for them both to 'enjoy' whilst watching the film! He didn't have the heart to tell her that he preferred sherbet ones! It proved a meaningful occasion in more ways than one. Not least because the film included the song 'Be My Love' bellowed out by Lanza and which summed up Wilf's feelings about Brenda to a tee but because it also became the song that earned Lanza his first gold record. Every one of Wilf's letters to his love affirmed his feelings for her and outlined his proposals and plans for their future lives together. One extra special note, carried by his tried and trusted courier, plucked up the courage to ask her to marry him and after watching 'The Toast of New Orleans' in the small picture palace on the Hill Brenda accepted.

When she became pregnant Wilf approached Archie, Brenda's father, as confidently as he could to politely ask him for his youngest daughter's hand in marriage. Archie was a small man whose face looked as if it had worn out two bodies, with wrinkles as deep as tramlines across both of his cheeks. He was rarely seen without a pipe full of baccie (tobacco), a snuffbox and a pint of ale in his hands. Within his small stature however hid the strength of a giant and because of this Wilf tentatively tiptoed around him at their pre-nuptial tryst. As it turned out, Wilf need not have felt anxious or worried about it at all. In truth, the meeting was nothing more than a formality. Archie had been unlikely to refuse anything or anyone in Brenda's condition and was thankful that shame would not be crossing his doorstep since Wilf was more than willing to make an honest woman out of his youngest wench. Liza, his wife, had enough troubles of her own without inheriting a bastard grandchild. She was however adamant that her youngest wench would not get married in a wedding dress and certainly not in anything that came anywhere close to being classified as white or cream. Brenda would have to choose a serviceable suit and one that had an elasticated waistband so that she could get a good few months wear out of it. And so, a speedy, small shotgun style wedding was arranged and conducted at Christ Church, High Street, Tunstall. It had to be 'done' in a church if it was to feel permanent, bonded and blessed in the eyes of God Almighty. And so on the 16 December 1950 Wilf and Brenda made their vows:

To have and to hold,   From this day forward,
For better, for worse,   For richer, for poorer
In sickness and in health,   To love and to cherish (and obey (Brenda only, of course!))
Till death us do part

in the presence of their immediate families, the vicar and, hopefully, God Himself.

* * *

Nell made her presence so blatantly obvious at the wedding that she stuck out like a bloody sore thumb. Instead of wearing a hat she decided to wear a face like a 'smacked arse' from the beginning of the day right up until the sun went down on it. Her grim, stern face never cracked a smile and, when she saw The Cake, her creation, appear re-iced as a wedding cake, if looks could have killed then the entire wedding party would have all dropped down bloody dead.

Nell had planned to return from Lancashire just as soon as she thought the dust had settled on events surrounding Kenneth's death. She was forced however to return home sooner than planned because the School Board Man had knocked loudly on her family's door to enquire why the children, and Alma in particular, were not attending school. None of the three children had been allowed to return to school at the start of the new academic year in September 1941. It was a good two months after Kenneth's death in early July and Alma, just eight, was 'kept-off' from school to wash, iron, cook and clean in her Mother's stead. Bill thought it to be the most sensible and simplest of solutions in Nell's absence and, in his mind, was an obvious natural decision in lieu of her presence. He was genuinely at a loss to understand what all the fuss was about. Sending out the School Board Man indeed! Alma was learning everything wenches needed to know about life and especially how to wash, iron, cook and clean. His children's absence from school and the avoidance of playground taunts served a double, and perhaps a more important, purpose. Not attending school restricted who the children spoke to about their raw recollections surrounding Kenneth's death and, in turn, protected them from the many questions and rumours that were still circulating around the village. The reasoning behind this decision was, that given enough time, everyone's memory of the tragedy would dim and when everything had died a natural death and people had forgotten the 'whys and wherefores' of it all the children would return safely to school and face the precarious playground pundits. But what Bill and Nell had not banked on in their carefully contrived plan was the School Board Man throwing a spanner in the works. In the end, there was nothing left for Bill to do other than to ask Nell to come home if only to enable the children to return to school in order get the authorities off his back. He could not chance the resurrection of an investigation and Nell would never agree to anyone, not even Elsie Williams, looking after her bairns and especially baby Terrence. After Nell arrived home from her Lancashire retreat Elsie never stopped asking her about her bairn. She was like a fly round muck! 'Would she like her to take Terrence out for a walk or watch him for a couple of hours for her? Would Nell like her to take him to the shops for a bit of fresh air while she did her washing? One day she even appeared at Nell's door with a baby blue knitted outfit wrapped in tissue paper as a gift for the pleasant little chap. Nell however did not take kindly to accepting what she perceived as charity. It went against her independent grain, although she remained polite in her responses to Elsie, being more than grateful to her for her kindness, Nell was not about to let Terrence out of her sight. She trusted no bugger anymore and thought that Elsie Williams had ulterior motives behind her so-called offers of help.

On her return home, Nell kept her head down for as long as she possibly could. Her philosophy, in this instance, was 'that if you didn't want your head blown off then you should keep it well below the parapets'. So she decided to keep a low profile and mind herself with her own bloody business. Keeping herself to herself was a mammoth task for Nell but was a means to an end. Every second of every day, she hoped and prayed that the dust surrounding Kenneth's death would settle down. She trusted in the commonly held belief that all rumours and innuendos were only a nine-day wonder and gossipers would soon become bored and move onto the next social scandal. It was however to prove a very long time before anything as juicy as Kenneth was discussed on street corners and whispered over backyard walls. Nell was determined to move forward and take what remained of her family with her. She never mentioned Kenneth's name to anyone and neither did any of her kith and kin dare to do so. He was dead and buried in every way, shape and form. If Nell was nothing else she was always true to her word and kept her promises both good and bad. For more reasons than one she had left Kenneth well and truly behind. She had no choice in the matter, she had to leave him behind and so must everyone else in her family.

* * *

Nell was not impressed at all by the hushed-up wedding of her biggest and eldest son and was never one to disguise her feelings of disapproval. Onlookers assumed that her displeasure was due to the loss of another one of her boys and her eldest one at that. Wilf however suspected that it was far less to do with losing another son and more to do with the loss of her son's earnings from the household budget that grieved her and was almost certainly at the bottom of her disparagement. Even if Wilf had brought the Queen of Sheba home for tea Nell would not have been pleased to meet her. She viewed all prospective wives purely as a threat to the family's income. Umbrage was written all over her face and it would be a long time before it melted away.

Her disapproval of the alliance first became apparent at Wilf's twenty-first birthday celebration in late October and just ahead of his marriage in December. Nell had been planning his twenty-first birthday for what seemed like a month of Sundays and, at last, the day arrived. She had known for some months that Wilf was walking out with Brenda and had seen him smuggling notes to Alma and vice versa. Whatever else she was Nell was not daft and neither was she bloody blind. Although she did not object to Brenda's presence at Wilf's coming of age celebration she devised devilish ways of keeping her well and truly at arm's length throughout the well rehearsed party. She did not want to inadvertently encourage her in any way. The memorable moment finally arrived. It was the culmination of many months of hard work. Nell slipped out of the small middle room and returned as fast as her legs would carry her with 'The Cake'. She had been making it and hiding it for weeks. Everyone stood and engulfed the small table. Bill felt as proud as a peacock as his chest expanded almost to bursting point. Alma, Billy and Terrence all stared in amazement and anticipation at The Cake. They had never seen anything quite like it before. Nell had certainly pulled out all the stops! What a treat they were in for. Their mouths watered at the thought of it. Wilf picked up the knife to cut through the icing that had cost Nell an arm and a leg. Everyone was excited, jubilant in every respect as laughter filled the air. The anticipation mounted. Wilf raised the knife to cut the cake. Silence fell as everyone watched and waited willing him to cut into the masterpiece   He suspended the knife in mid-air and, quite unexpectedly, paused. He had planned to make an announcement and make an announcement he would. There was no time like the present especially because he didn't believe in putting off 'til tomorrow what you could do today.

He cleared his throat.   Brenda sensed, almost instantaneously, that he intended to divulge their secret and set the record straight as he half-jokingly toyed:

"Well now, this cake looks too good to cut into and eat. Don't you all agree? In fact, I think we should save it for a very special occasion."

Total confusion filled the room. Everyone looked at everyone else. Nell, perhaps for the first time in her life, was dumbstruck. She had been expecting a short speech expressing gratitude to her, her family and Her Cake. She didn't know whether to laugh, surely he was having a joke, or cry. 'He was pulling their legs, wasn't he?' she thought.

Wilf quite slowly and deliberately put down the knife and laid it to rest alongside The Cake. At twenty-one he could do and say what he'd a mind to. No bugger could stop him now and if he no longer chose to turn up his wages to his Mother and be given a pittance of pocket money in return then he wouldn't have to. He could pay her board and lodgings instead. Lots of other blokes seemed to do that when they hit the magic twenty-one. He had become a man overnight and was even old enough to vote in the next general election. With all these thoughts rushing through his mind Wilf extended his right hand and arm towards his love and beckoned her forward to take her rightful place alongside him. Brenda for most of the time had been well and truly relegated to the corner of the room. Occasionally she had peeped round one or another of Wilf's family in order to catch a glimpse of the frivolities of the party spirit rather like a punter in the cheapest of theatre seats. She was, after all an outsider, an intruder within this tight family circle and Nell ensured that she sent out that message loud and clear and that Brenda fully understood it. So, thankful to be there at all, Brenda had succumbed to her place on its perimeter but Wilf was having none of it. Pulling his shrinking violet towards him he boldly declared:

"I would like to introduce you to my fiancée, my future wife and mother of my children, Brenda." They both stood together, centre stage leaving the audience aghast. Wilf scanned the room, eyeballing his family one-by-one, trying to absorb each of their shocked expressions in turn. Brenda turned as red as a ripe tomato and lowered her head, half out of embarrassment and half in resignation to her situation. Everyone in the room guessed, in that very instant, that Brenda was pregnant. Nell was furious. She would not be taken for any bugger's fool and immediately snatched up The Cake from off the middle of the table and returned it to its hiding place. Anyone would have thought it was the Great Star of Africa diamond as she carefully locked it away and threatened that it would never see the light of day again. She vowed never to make another bloody cake for any of her ungrateful sods. After that little episode the party did not go with a bang but rather went down like a big lead balloon.

In fact, The Cake, Nell's cake, made for Wilf's special birthday, was saved, re-iced, redressed and reappeared, to Nell's disgust, as a wedding cake at their succinct and somewhat sober family celebration.

* * *

Wilf did not chose a 'best man' to stand alongside him on his wedding day and to keep Brenda's thinnest of 9carat gold bands safe until, with the words, 'with this ring I thee wed' he placed it on the third finger of her left hand. He stood alone at the front of the church. 'How could he possibly have chosen any other man to stand with him? His best man, his brother, was dead' he reasoned. The cold comfort, if there was any comfort at all, was in the fact that the responsibilities and legalities expected of him when, overnight, he had become a man, would not be onerous or new to him. He had carried the burden of responsibility, especially for Kenneth's death, since he was almost twelve years old. In fact, he had felt twenty-one years of age for a very, very long time.

As he stood alone waiting for Archie to walk his young bride down the aisle his almost twelve yet twenty-one year-old heart still yearned and longed for his younger brother. A brother who should have been nineteen years old, standing alongside him, shoulder to shoulder, in the role of his best man on this his wedding day. No one had taken his brother's place and no one ever would.

CHAPTER EIGHT –
THE LESSER OF TWO EVILS

The newly married couple took up residence in a rented upstairs room, not a house or an apartment, just one room within a small already overcrowded house. Apart from their personal belongings everything else in the house was shared. The kitchen was constantly occupied and Brenda found herself clearing away and cleaning up after everyone and their dog. It was a sad and dismal introduction to married life. When they were looking for somewhere to live they had not only taken what they could find but also what they could afford and that hadn't been very much at all. As the tell tale signs of pregnancy became more apparent Brenda worried how she would cope with motherhood and what life would be like, living in squalor, when the baby came. To say that the house was dirty would have been an understatement of fact because filthy would have best described it. There wasn't enough room to turn around in the solitary room they tried their utmost to call home.

Soon after their marriage Wilf took employment in one of the local coalmines in an attempt to escape conscription into the armed forces but, in the end, he could not stomach the claustrophobia and dirt of the pit. He detested it and could not get rid of the taste of coal dust. He consumed it with every bite of food and every swallow of liquid and yet still the taste of it lingered. It could not be washed away and clung to him, so much so, that he never felt clean. Rumour had it that the Kidsgrove Boggart or, as the miners liked to call her the Kid Crew Bugget, a local ghost in the form of a headless woman in white, who haunted the area and gave warning of forthcoming pit disasters, had recently been seen by a number of witnesses. Sightings of her were said to indicate that a pit disaster, according to the superstitious, was imminent. Legend had it that the woman had been murdered whilst travelling through one of the many canal tunnels designed by the famous engineer James Brindley who lived and died in the local community. A boatman was caught, convicted and hanged for the woman's murder but the ghost's eerie sightings sent shivers through the local mines and down the backs of the biggest and strongest of men. Wilf, on the other hand, didn't lay much store by stories of ghosts. His Mother always told him, in no uncertain terms, that 'it was the living ya needed to be afraid of, not the bloody dead'. The thought of a cave-in, however, undoubtedly unnerved him. He did not fancy being buried alive. He eventually and somewhat reluctantly came to the pragmatic conclusion that nothing could be worse than being crushed into a cage and dropped deep into the ground to work like a rat in claustrophobic coffin-like tunnels oblivious to whether it was night or day up top. He opted for what he thought would be the lesser of two evils and entered the Royal Engineers as a Lance Corporal on 17 May 1951 just over a month before the birth of his first child.

In his absence Brenda went to live with Nell, Bill, Alma, Billy and Terrence in their two up and two and a half down terraced house in Golden Hill. Initially, Nell was delighted by the arrangement. She was a dab hand at changing her tune and regurgitating sayings to match her personal situation and stance. 'Every cloud has a silver lining' she cheerily declared to Brenda as she warmly welcomed her into the cramped fold. Rather like an invitation from a spider to a fly. Secretly however Nell could not help thinking that 'there was always more ways than one of digging for money'. Wilf had agreed to send her a large cut from his army pay packet to care for Brenda and his child when it arrived. How Brenda longed to return to the familiarity of her own home and her own Mother, Liza, and her Father, Archie, but in reality it was out of the question and had never really been an option. There was no room at that inn for Brenda and her unborn child. Her parents still used a Duckett toilet with a wooden board covering its cesspit and despite being regularly emptied it still stank to high heaven. She was therefore left with no choice, especially with a bairn on the way, other than to find an unassuming and inconspicuous place within Nell's household. She shared a bed with Alma, her sister-in-law and ex-courier, and waited for the return of her sapper soldier husband. Although she had only been married for five months she trusted that on his return he would find them a house and she would turn it into a home. A home meant so much more than simply having a roof over their heads and Brenda longed to feather her own cosy nest and create a home that would feel blessed in every respect.

Probably the only thing she found herself grateful for at this time in her life was the auspicious birth of the National Health Service. It had been a long time coming but Nye Bevan and his boys made their dream of free healthcare at the point of need a reality on 5 July 1948 and the nation, apart from a large percentage of doctors, breathed a huge sigh of relief at its inauguration. 'What did it matter to people like Brenda that Bevan was forced to stuff the doctors' mouths with gold in order to get his bill through parliament?' What really mattered, to women and children who had suffered the most horrendous neglect purely because they had not been insured and unable to pay for medical care, was the implementation of Bevan's dream of free health care for all from the cradle to the grave. The system became the envy of the world. The fact that Brenda was cared for by qualified medical staff under the NHS turned out to be a double blessing since it saved her the embarrassment of enduring Nell's prodding and probing of her pregnant private parts! In spite of her objections Nell still insisted on 'taking a look' at Brenda on more than one occasion. Not everyone, for very different reasons, was altogether happy with the concept of the newly formed Ministry of Health and the free for all tripartite system of health care.

Wilf's assumptions about the armed forces being the lesser of two evils could not have been farther from the truth. Up until this episode in his life Wilf had never left the confines of his own country; not even to cross the English Channel. Far too soon, in far too many respects, he found himself ordered into armed combat in the Korean War. Fear, since the loss of his brother, had never ceased to simmer in the back of his mind, but here, in the thick of war, She raised her ugly and terrible head in a very different but equally intense and sinister way. He said that you could smell Her. Fear's stench emanated from every pore in every square inch of skin squashed into every dugout and if his accounts were to be believed no man ever went over the top of a trench as an atheist. He surmised that 'everybody believed in something, even if they chose to believe in nothing, because believing in nothing was in itself, still a belief'. During this time, a bible, along with other essential items, was provided as standard issue to service personnel. Although not a religious man, Wilf had a special place in his heart for bibles. This reverence emerged as a result of events on a solemn day in 1941 when he was asked to collect a prize, a Holy Bible, awarded posthumously to Kenneth in recognition of his attendance at Sunday school during the year of his death. It fell to Wilf, as the eldest sibling, to accept the award on Kenneth's behalf. Within the front cover on the first page of the special book was written:

'Awarded to Kenneth Hackney
for regular and punctual attendance at
Golden Hill Methodist Sunday School 1941'

So Wilf had two bibles, one might say a double portion, into which he pinned his faith, hope and trust believing, in an almost childlike way, that they would bring him safely through the storms of war. He was not alone in his bargaining pleas and prayers for a safe return home. Men who had never put a foot inside a church found themselves expressing something akin to a faith in God. At times of desperation grown men, of every description, felt compelled to appeal to a divine authority to help and save them. The unstinting work of the Salvation Army who, according to Wilf, could be found delivering all kinds of sustenance to troops, in all kinds of life-threatening situations, promoted belief in something if only human kindness. Wilf discovered that expressing even a small degree of faith helped to combat and overcome the taunts and terrors of Fear herself. Faith seemed, albeit temporarily, to silence her snide remarks. The army of chaplains also played their vital part in an unbelievable living hell. They brushed shoulders with Death whilst attempting to bring spiritual comfort to the living and a measure of peace to the dying. They stood alongside their comrades and were integral parts of the combined war effort. They could be heard reading aloud, sometimes shouting above the noise, the most comforting of bible passages whilst conducting communion services in the thickest dirt, debris and decay.

Separation was extremely hard for all the recruits during the Korean War and Wilf, like so many other boys, kept photographs of his sweetheart and his first-born daughter close to his heart. Perhaps unique to him,

Wilf protected his images within the pages of his brother's bible. By the light of an oil lamp and with the sounds of war pounding in his head and heart he penned words of promise and hope to his young wife:

'God blessed us with a daughter fair,
He cannot answer every prayer,
So keep good faith, my darling Wife,
We'll soon be together for the rest of our life'.

He sent these words to Brenda together with four Japanese silk handkerchiefs each embroidered with messages of affection and love. One simply said:

'I LOVE YOU' and another 'REMEMBER ME'.

Wilf had paid for the handkerchiefs by trading in some of his ration allowance in exchange for them. He carefully folded each one, placed them with his letter and poem and sent them to his sweetheart, his wife, his Brenda May. As soon as the envelope was sealed and posted, Wilf started to save his rations up again to buy a photograph album and a musical box. By volunteering for extra duties he saved enough money to buy his Japanese gifts which travelled every mile back with him on his long journey home.

During his time in Korea Wilf was fortunate enough to hitch a lift with some of his American comrades in order to visit Japan and became immediately enthralled and fascinated by the country's culture. In spite of the ravages of war he described his perception of her as both beautiful and breathtaking. He was particularly overwhelmed by one of Japan's three holy mountains, Mount Fuij, the highest mountain in Japan on Honshu Island about 62 miles (100 kms) south west of Tokyo. From Yokohama, on a very clear day, Wilf gazed upon Fuij's snow-capped tranquil beauty, almost absorbed by a sense of timelessness and genuine peace before being consumed again by the ever-present pain and realities of war. Japan was a real eye-opening experience and one he would never forget. He watched looked and listened as, during thunderstorms, some children tried to hide their belly buttons. He came to understand that this behaviour was accredited to Raijin, a god of thunder, lightning and storms found within the Shinto religion and Japanese mythology. Folk belief taught that Raijin had sometimes been credited with eating the navels or stomachs of children and because of this some children traditionally fell on their faces and stomachs in order to hide them during a storm in fear that this might happen to them.

Wilf also never forgot the grace, serenity and beauty of Geisha girls and talked not only of their outward mesmerising and compelling appearance but also their inner unlimited beauty and strength; their very nature and demeanour. He deduced that such an unimaginable level of inner grace and way of being could probably have been accredited to their origin and preparation for Geisha life. He learned that girls were destined to become Geisha from a very early age. Some reports indicated that girls as young as five or six had their feet broken, remoulded and bound in an attempt to keep their feet small enough to fit into the tiniest of shoes because eligibility was judged on the shape and size of a girl's feet.

This practice also prepared them to wear huge Geisha platform shoes that equally emphasised both femininity and weakness. Their use of makeup was fascinating and their attention to detail immaculate. Hair clips, often in the shape of butterflies, were an outward adornment indicative of the transformation that had taken place in their lives.

During this enforced chapter, an almost interlude in Wilf's life, one of his enduring memories, among so many, was undoubtedly the short story of Madame Butterfly by Amercian writer John Luther Long. The story unwraps the memories of John's sister, Jennie Correll, whose husband was a Methodist missionary in Japan in the late nineteenth century. The libretto of Giacomo Puccini's opera Madame Butterfly is based in part on this short story in addition to elements that were also derived from the novel Madame Chrysatheme by Pierre Loti. It is widely believed that the story of the opera was based on actual events that occurred in Nagasaki in the early 1890s. Wilf never tired of listening to One Fine Day, from Madame Butterfly, the beguiling and beautiful little Butterfly aria.

Before leaving Korea, Wilf planned, by hook or by crook to visit the newly constructed War Cemetery in Hodogaya, Yokohama. The cemetery, located about nine kilometres west of central Yokohama, was constructed in 1945 by the Australian War Graves Group after the second-world war and contained the graves of Commonwealth servicemen who died in Japan as prisoners of war or with the occupation after the war. It

101

comprises four main sections; Australian, Canadian, New Zealand, United Kingdom and the Indian forces (1939-1945) section. Wilf determined to visit the cemetery not only as an act of remembrance but also to demonstrate his own personal act of honour to every one of the World War II related burials and commemorations to soldiers, sailors, airmen and merchant fleet personnel who died as prisoners of war in or near Japan. He also discovered a post World War II area for the graves of those who died of illness or accident and also for those who had died or who would die following military service in the Korean War. As captivating and as beautiful as Japan was Wilf did not like to think that his bones might be buried so very far away from home. He humbly acknowledged that he would never forget the lives of those who were buried there and would always wear a poppy with pride as a symbol of remembrance and respect. He longed, more than ever, like so many others alongside him, to find his way home, back to his family, to his wife and his daughter; his own little butterfly. As he saluted his comrades of the past and bowed his head in humility before the memorials of those who had paid the ultimate price for his freedom his thoughts instinctively turned towards his brother Kenneth and, in that foreign land so far away from home, he was overwhelmingly conscious that he had never stood at his own brother's graveside since the day he had been buried; not once, never. He reasoned he had obeyed his mother to the letter in this respect. Yet his reasoning did not hold water and carried no weight. He knew the truth of the matter only too well. How could he ever have visited his brother's grave?

He had caused his death and nothing would ever change that no matter how many miles away from home he was.

Wilf kept his discharge records received from whole-time military service and saved them alongside his medals one of which was awarded 'For service in the defence of the principles of the Charter of the United Nations'. He saw them as recognition, an endorsement, and one of equal value whether earned by a former grammar school or secondary school boy. There was no differentiation in this type of acknowledgment and he felt humbled by his country's appreciation of his loyalty and service.

After being demobbed from national service in May 1953 his military conduct reported him as having been 'Very Good' and went on to record: "Wilf has served his country in Korea in field engineering tasks. He is intelligent, hard working and possesses initiative. He can manage a team of men and is capable of organising work. Is smart, sober and honest. Has always remained calm and cheerful under conditions of danger and acute discomfort."

His struggles did not magically come to an end after his discharge from national service although he secured employment and moved into a new council house with an inside toilet and bathroom of its very own; luxuries indeed. He had well and truly landed on his feet!

Brenda and Wilf were blessed the following year, in April 1954, with the gift of another daughter, Angela, so named because she reminded Wilf of an angel. A blonde haired baby, in contrast to their first-born whose dark eyes and hair favoured her Father's features. The daughters were poles apart in terms of looks and characteristics, rather like Wilf and Kenneth, but were both equally valued, cherished and loved. Wenches had their place. They could always help with the domestic duties. In time Brenda would teach 'em how to manage a home and juggle the biggest of families on the smallest and tightest of budgets. Although he loved them both beyond expression Wilf secretly longed for a son and, be it a humble heritage, an heir. A boy who would bear his name and in time hopefully secure his lineage.

The little family moved into another two bedroom semi-detached council house during the autumn of 1955 which was closer to where Wilf had grown up. On his return from Korea he had tried his best to settle into another area, just a few miles away from where he had been born and bred. He missed the familiarity and camaraderie of a small, close-knit community with its ever-ready offers of help, stubborn independence and resolute resilience. The downside of moving closer to home was the reality that it would prove impossible not to relive the best and the worst of his memories and only time would tell if this consequence would prove to be a blessing or a curse.

The house was positioned on the corner of two streets affording it a larger than average garden. The day after the family moved into the house Wilf started to build a large wooden fence all the way round the garden's perimeter. This not only kept people out but more importantly, kept his children in and therefore hopefully safe. He understood that children needed to play but they had each other for that, especially two wenches. He planted a number of old saggars, left by the previous tenant, with violets, marigolds, bluebells and London pride. Saggars, fireclay containers, mostly oval or round were made and used by the local pottery industries to hold and protect pottery from being marked by flames and smoke during firing in the bottle ovens. After production all new saggars were fired in the kiln and expected to have a life span of about thirty to forty firings. This estimation always assumed that they did not break or chip first. Rather than discard the worn out saggars they were sometimes filled with flowers and lined up together to form a colourful makeshift wall. Wilf's work did not end with the planting of flowers in saggars. He had a list of jobs as long as his arm but decided to prioritise the excavation of the half-buried corrugated Anderson shelter still in-situ at the bottom of their newly acquired garden. The shelter had its own distinctive and musty smell, an unpleasant place with an equally unpleasant aura about it. Had the shelter had a voice then it would surely have had many tales to tell of things seen and heard throughout the war years. Its presence however resurrected unwelcome memories of the Morrison shelter with its cage-like mesh sides into which Wilf and his family had crawled like dogs scurrying underneath a table to hide. The shelter at his new home definitely had to go and in its place he planned to sow a vegetable patch. He didn't need any triggers to help him to remember anything. He knew, only too well, that there were some things he would never be able to forgive or forget.

By securing a position at the local iron and steel works Wilf completed a full circle and landed back where he had first started out from working alongside his Father Bill, his brother-in-law Alan (Alma's husband) and his brother Terrence at the local foundry. He quickly gained ground and a degree of notoriety and respect. Known for being a straight-laced and outspoken man who wasn't afraid of calling a spade a spade and, because of such traits, he was unanimously appointed as Shop Steward. He had a voice worth listening to and one that was not afraid of white-collared workers. He wanted to change the world and started by speaking out from the confines of his union role against injustice and fat cats who lined their even fatter pockets with the cream of the industry made off the backs of hard-working men. Men who simply wanted a fair day's pay for a fair day's labour in order to keep food on their tables and clothes on the backs of their children. The seeds of his strong political principles had been sown in his heart during hushed parleys with his brother Kenneth and, in a roundabout way, they had found their way to the surface of his life and were at last bearing fruit.

During his lunch breaks he worked to forge a garden swing from the various remnants of iron and steel he retrieved and purchased from off the slagheap. He melted, smelted and shaped it, section-by-section, bolt-by-bolt until it became perfect. At its investiture in his corner-plot garden the swing was painted green and had a much stronger than necessary heavy-duty chain enabling it to cradle a huge double sized seat, purposely designed to hold at least two of his children at the same time. Rather like a bicycle made for two only in this instance it was a custom-made swing that, at a squash, could hold three little 'uns. 'No need for my bairns to go and play in the playground now' he thought to himself. He had created one within the parameters of his own garden fence. Wilf needed his children to be exactly where he could see them and where he could make damn sure that they would always be safe. The fence served as a bulwark eliminating the risk of any of his little 'uns wandering off outside the security of its boundary and ending up lost or hurt or worse. He was determined not to lose another one of his family. His brother was enough of a loss to last him a bloody lifetime and he would not be, he could not be, responsible for the death of another child.

CHAPTER NINE - CHRISTMAS 1956

Christmas Eve 1956 found Angela, closer to three than two, and Vivien five and a half, hoping for dollies, a chocolate smoker's outfit, a Christmas stocking filled with sweets, fruit, nuts and if they were really lucky, a shiny new three-penny bit. In reality, their Christmas stockings were just a pair of Wilf's working socks that had been dressed-up to resemble special Christmas ones.

It had started to snow early in the morning on Christmas Eve and by teatime Brenda was pacing the floor holding her back. She paused periodically to grip the edge of the table until the contractions passed their peak.

"They will slow, they will pass" she muttered. "Not today, not on Christmas Eve! We won't have a cat in hell's chance of getting a midwife today, a good flurry of snow an' all!" Frances, her kind-hearted next-door neighbour, had promised that she would knock on the midwife's door when she passed it on her way to collect their Christmas goose and ask her to pop down to check on Brenda; but that was before the heavens opened and it started to bucket down humungous snowflakes.

Brenda could not help thinking that it was all very well listening to Bing Crosby crooning out 'I'm Dreaming of a White Christmas' because it wasn't bloody him who was in bloody labour on Christmas Eve. Snow was all very well on Christmas cards and for looking out at from the inside of shiny windows, a warm hearth and a full belly but why, dear God, had it got to snow today when she was obviously in the early stages of labour.

Wilf, practically frozen solid, almost fell in through the back door of his home after the end of a double-shift at the foundry. He normally cycled the five miles each way to work and back every day. He found it far cheaper than giving the Bus Company his hard-earned brass even though it resulted in an almost full-time job repairing punctures. He was often found with an inner tube immersed in a bowl of water watching for the telltale signs of a hole in the tube wall. Once he spotted the bubbles he carefully dried the tube, marked it with white chalk before applying a plaster to the hole from his small tin box containing his precious puncture kit. How long the patch would actually last for was anybody's guess. Some of his inner tubes had more plaster on 'em than a broken leg. He was admittedly his own worst enemy when it came to punctures. On more than one occasion he devilishly held onto the back of a lorry and freewheeled half way home over the roughest ground imaginable and, in so doing, incurred many a flat tyre. Such antics enabled him to beat the bus with its unending stopping and starting and became a worthwhile endeavour simply because he arrived home all the earlier giving him more time for what really mattered in life, his family. Work was a means to an end and Wilf worked to live and never lived to work.

As he entered the small kitchen Brenda was bent over two-double in labour. "It's comin' Wilf. Fetch us the midwife. It's comin'" she screamed. Having just finished wading through what was to be the start of the worst blizzard in years and having pushed his bike more than riding it on the treacherous journey home he knew he would not be leaving the house again even in search of a midwife. More than once he had thought he would never have made it home for Christmas so to brave the elements again and risk being separated from his family was out of the question. He would not leave his love when she needed him. In fact, wild horses would not drag him from her side. 'Had he not helped his Mother, Nell, to deliver a bairn when there was nobody else to help?' he reasoned. 'Had he not seen many a bitch birth her pups?' the interrogation went on in an attempt to reassure himself, more than anyone else, about what he needed to do.

Without wasting a second he ran up the stairs two at a time in more than half a-frenzy as the adrenaline pumped at superfast speed round his body. He was so energetic that nobody in their right mind would have believed he had just finished a double-shift and cycled home through nearly ten foot of snow. He moved as quick as Jack Flash and as fast as any other comic book hero as he started to dismantle their very old and very solid double bed. Nuts, washers and bolts came off like lightning. He carried down the top and bottom boards first, followed by the springs, which although folded in half, still hit every stair on their way down as he roughly pulled, pushed and guided them as best he could. Lastly, he gave the mattress an almighty push over the top of the landing resulting in it finding its own way down the wooden hills and landing butt up to the front door in the red-tiled pokey porch. He did not stop for a breath. Brenda and the girls looked on in amazement. He stoked up the fire and put pans of water and cloths around the gas stove. Had Brenda not been in so much pain she might have objected to the enforced arrangement but she resigned herself to the situation and let him get on with it. Her Wilf always knew what to do in a crisis. This was one of the advantages of being the eldest sibling in his family. He went into automatic mode and took control of situations, acting on, and using his own initiative. 'Wasn't that what his discharge report had said?' Brenda found herself thinking until a strong contraction eradicated all such thoughts from her mind. Wilf's positive attributes were, of course, finely balanced against the overwhelming sense of responsibility that ensued after his actions went askew. If he was truly in charge of a situation, then there was no one else to blame other than himself when events turned terribly wrong. He knew, only too well, what it felt like to have the buck stop at his door. Today, though, he would make no mistakes. He was sure he knew exactly what to do in the situation. Another child, his child, was coming into the world and he already knew that he would move heaven and earth for it.

Once the bed had been set up in the small living room aside a roaring fire Wilf tried to encourage Brenda into it whilst, at the same time, he whisked Angela up in his right arm and grasped Vivien's hand with his left. The girls, though dazed by such unusual events, were both totally absorbed with their Christmas expectations. Brenda had occupied and distracted them all day by showing them, among other things, how to stick together strips of coloured paper to make colourful daisy-like chains. As soon as a chain was long enough to form a streamer the girls set about draping it around the room in the most unlikely of places and Brenda suddenly noticed one draped across the bed head. 'Dear God' she thought. 'Am I really going to give birth to a baby with a bloody streamer stuck on top of my piggin' head?'

The girls had also, in a fashion, decorated the bottom half of the tree with striped candy canes, pink and white sugar mice and a new set of pear shaped coloured lights. A worse for wear dishevelled Christmas angel was left lying on the chair arm waiting for Wilf's long arms to place her in pride of position on top of the tree. Vivien, somewhat oblivious to the momentous occasion, continued half humming and half singing as much as she could remember of:

C is for the Candy trim around the Christmas tree,
H is for the Happiness in all the family,
R is for the Reindeer prancing by the windowpane,
I is for the Icing on the cake as sweet as sugar cane,
S is for the Stockings on the chimney wall,
T is for the Toys beneath the tree so tall,

M is for the Mistletoe where everyone gets kissed,
A is for the Angels who make up the Christmas lists and
S is for old Santa who makes every kid his pet.
Be good and He'll bring you everything in your Christmas Alphabet.

So when her Father almost sternly said: "Time to get ready for Santa Claus; tonight is a very special night", neither of the girls resisted or complained but Vivien, unaware of what was really happening hesitated slightly and asked him the most important of questions: "Will you put Angel Gabriel on top of the tree Dad please, please? She implored. "She needs to be where everyone can see her." Without a moment's hesitation Wilf placed the unkempt angel on top of the tree where, quite conversely, she immediately had a bird's eye view and would hopefully watch over everything and everyone in the room. He quickly wiped their faces with a warm cloth before taking them over to the streamer-strewn bed to kiss their Mother goodnight and Vivien asked: "Can you see her Mum? Can you see Angel Gabriel?"

"Yes, I can see her" Brenda replied in between contractions. "She looks beautiful". Wilf felt sure he had heard Angel Gabriel referred to in the male tense. 'But what did it matter? An angel was an angel wasn't it?' he concluded and without further ado he took both of his very own angels upstairs to bed.

"Be quiet now" he said as he swiftly tucked them up. "Night and Bless. Sleep tight and tomorrow when you wake up Santa will have been and left you some presents". He shut the bedroom door firmly behind him.

So with thoughts of dollies and sweeties Vivien and Angela fell asleep into a night that would be the most special of Christmas Eves and one that would bring Wilf, the most precious Christmas gift of all.

Early in the morning of 25 December 1956, as the snow fell deep outside his palace of a council house and the fire roared up the chimney Wilf held the warm tiny body of his new born son in his calloused, hard-working hands as he whispered the name that had not been spoken aloud for over fifteen years: "Kenneth, his name is Kenneth".

He held up his baby boy in his fully extended arms as if to introduce him to the most special of Christmas Days. Whether he felt the need to do this in recognition, appreciation or submission to some unseen force or higher power he was not sure but deep in his heart he knew that Christmas Day was also known as the Saviour's Day. The day when the Son of God was born in a manger and peace and goodwill had been proclaimed to all men everywhere. It was on this day, the most special of all days, that Kenneth, his son was born and Wilf acknowledged the greatness of the gift as he lifted him up as high into the air as he possibly could. He had heard that the literal Italian translation of the words 'to give birth' were 'dara alla luce' which means 'to give or welcome to the light' and perhaps this beautiful thought influenced him as his emotions overwhelmed him. He had believed, in moments of deepest guilt and condemnation, that God, if there was one, would never have trusted him with another boy, but, on Christmas Day 1956 he held his son, God's most gracious gift of all in his arms. He could barely believe it himself and thought his heart would burst with joy.

He said that he must have felt something akin to the downcast bank manager portrayed by James Stuart in the Christmas film 'It's a Wonderful Life' not least because it was Christmas and life felt miraculously wonderful but also because the family had their own unique Angel Gabriel who had watched over the night's events and who even had a pair of well-earned worse-for-wear wings.

As he drew the babe back to himself and nestled his new born son in his strong arms he whispered the name 'Kenneth' again and silently promised to protect him with his life. He vowed that he would not let anything happen to him. He could speak out the name Kenneth as many times as he wanted to now and everyone else, including his Mother, would have to do the same. It felt as if the curse, if there was a curse at all, surrounding his brother's death had been broken and concurrently a large invisible glacier, in his almost twelve year-old heart cracked and started to melt. Momentarily he allowed himself the indulgence of wondering if he had been given a perfectly timed gift of a child, a son, on Christmas Day as a tangible message of divine forgiveness. He exhaled as he sensed relief, be it temporarily, flood through his entire body. Sadly, however he discovered that just like Hydra, the multi-headed snake, when one of Fear's heads is cut off another quickly grows back to replace it. No sooner had he held up his son in his strong arms of blessing, security and safety, no sooner had the iceberg started to melt within his heart than one breath from the ice cold lips of Fear re-froze and resealed the crack as She snidely whispered in his ear:

"You'd better protect this Kenneth with your life, with your whole being. Not like the first one, your brother, remember, the one who you let die".

He would never be free of the guilt he felt surrounding his brother's death and yet in spite of that he had been given the gift of a son which, in that moment in time, meant more to him than the world itself. A man could not buy such joy. It could not be purchased and was not exclusive to the rich and famous. He had been given the most precious of gifts on this the most precious of days and he would cherish and protect him with his life.

Just as soon as Brenda had sufficiently recovered from the traumatic birth Wilf booked the christening at the Methodist Chapel he had attended as a boy; the chapel where the funeral of his brother had taken place and the one where he had posthumously received the award of his bible.

The christening was arranged and the Godparents chosen. Not that there was really any choosing to be done. Who else would the Godparents have been other than Wilf's sister Alma and his brothers Billy and young Terrence? Everyone was dressed in what was to remain their Sunday best clothes for a very long time. Pride had, on more than one occasion, been forced onto the back burner in favour of practicality. Second hand clothes were usually purchased from local jumble sales, and if considered to be in 'good enough shape', were saved for Sunday best use only. Brenda had an eye for hand knitted jumpers and cardigans and would unpick and unravel the wool stitch-by-stitch and row-by-row. She then set about knitting the wool back up again making it into cardigans and jumpers for the children. She often boasted that she could make three children's cardigans from one man's sweater. Even the buttons, zips and press-studs were cut off and reused on the 'new' garments. The only time new clothes were bought was for Charity Sundays, the Chapel's anniversary days when the Methodists paraded through the village in their best of clothes, singing hymns on street corners and collecting money for charity. The christening of their son Kenneth felt ten times more important to them than all the Charity Sundays put together and as such deserved and demanded the smartest new clothes that their little money could buy.

Brenda ordered and almost spent a ten pound Provident cheque apart from a very small amount that was left in credit on it. She hoped to combine the balance with the few pennies that remained on previous cheques safely stored in the kitchen drawer. With all the pittances combined she hoped that she would have enough credit to buy a pair of sand coloured seamless nylons but to do so she would first have to brave the shop assistant's attitude towards her. It always proved embarrassing to stand opposite the perfectly made-up assistant while she rolled her eyes, let out a huge sigh and reluctantly and lazily reckoned up all the balances on the numerous cheques. Brenda was relieved when she saw her reach into a drawer and pull out a packet of nylons before slapping them down on the counter and grudgingly passing them to her without a paper bag. Brenda had little or no alternative other than to weather the embarrassment. Her only other option would have been to wear a stocking with a small ladder in it. Although she was a dab hand at manoeuvring the stocking round so that the ladder appeared on the inside rather than on the outside of her leg the ladder would still run. The only thing to stop it dead in its tracks would be a dab of nail varnish and she didn't own any of that! Nail polish was far too expensive and far too extravagant to even consider as a viable option. No, the ladder would have ended up looking like a bloody tramline and been impossible to hide no matter how hard she tried to twist it round her leg. So, although very restricted in her choice of clothes, because not many shops displayed the 'Provident Accepted Here' symbol, she managed to do a wonderful job of kitting them all out. She hardly spared a thought for the eleven pounds, including interest, she would have to repay to the Provident Company over the next twenty-one weeks in order to repay this form of loan. She had a good relationship with the friendly local Provie agent who lived in the very next street. Brenda always coughed up her weekly payments on time and had never pretended not to be in when she heard her rap loudly on the front door to collect money. In fact, Brenda was almost unique in this respect as sometimes the agent's customers hid in the pantry on collection day in an attempt to convince her that the house was empty. Their avoidance plans were often scuppered as children, and especially babies, could not comprehend the meaning of 'hush be quiet, please be quiet, just for a minute'. Invariably the collector got wind of them hiding in the pantry and knocked all the louder and longer until the occupants were forced, out of embarrassment, to answer the door. All manner of agents and collectors could be seen and heard knocking on the small pantry windows of the council estate whilst shouting:

"I know you're in there, so you may as well open the door because I'm not going until you do. You haven't paid for three weeks on the trot so I'm not going until you answer the door and cough up." No, Brenda paid her dues on the nail and even up front on some occasions.

The girls were dressed in identical powder blue outfits and even had pillbox style hats with matching little handbags to complete their early spring outfits. Brenda and Wilf both wore suits and Brenda, in her new pair of nylons, did not have to worry about ladders as big as tramlines. A button had however at the eleventh hour pinged off one of her suspenders so she improvised by using a bit of cardboard in its place to hold her stocking up and prevent it from falling down. Alma had married on St Patrick's Day 17 March the year before and was earning good money working as a fully trained lithographer at a local Pot Bank. She always endeavoured to look smart and pulled out all the stops for this most special of days. Young Bill and Terence, both not to be outdone, were dressed up like dog's dinners in the suits they had worn for their sister's wedding the year before. What a proud picture they all looked as they walked together up to the chapel on top of the Hill.

Wilf carried Kenneth up the steps and in through the big wooden doors of the Wesleyan Chapel. For a brief moment, he seemed unable to overcome the unwanted flashbacks of the most awful of days when he had walked behind the coffin of his brother. He quickly looked down into his arms and into the face of his son Kenneth and determined, there and then, by the grace of God, that nothing would rob him of the moment. Guilt and Grief had not been invited but had turned up anyway and, no doubt, were both dressed in their finest array, as they inhabited a corner of the chapel. Wilf refused to acknowledge them but sensed them looking over his shoulder throughout the entire proceedings. Wherever he went and whatever he did sooner or later he became conscious of their presence. Sitting in the front pews again, he fixed his eyes like flint on the highly polished yet very plain cross at the front of the church, as he held Kenneth, his son, to his heart.

'Nothing would happen to this one. He'd see to that' he thought and yet his most vehement vow became clouded by what he thought to be the eeriest and strangest of coincidences. As the tune for the first hymn bellowed out from the piped organ it shook through every bone in his body.

The congregation stood and started to sing:

All things bright and beautiful
All creatures' great and small
All things wise and wonderful
The Lord God made them all.

It was one of the hymns that had been sung at his brother Kenneth's funeral. Fortunately however throughout the singing baby Kenneth became restless and was passed around the small baptism party proving a good distraction to the memories and emotions associated with the hymn.

As Wilf watched Brenda pass their bairn, their boy, to the minister to be baptised he thought his heart would burst with pride and joy.

"I baptise you Kenneth Roy in the name of the Father, the Son and the Holy Spirit" the minister said with true warmth and sincerity. He had been told a little of the family's tragic history and wanted to make the christening as meaningful as possible. In fact, the minister described the day as a healing balm for the painful past and an ointment for invisible wounds. Wilf remembered thinking that there could not possibly be enough ointment in the world to soothe and heal his wounds and pain. And anyway, the minister did not know the truth behind the tragedy. Nobody really did.

In spite of everything, including the tinges of sadness, the christening proved to be a 'red letter day' if ever there was one. Such excitement and joy was contagious. Later that day, friends and family well and truly wet the baby's head as they all celebrated with genuine joy and happiness.   Nobody who wanted to be there was excluded.   This was one of the best things that had ever happened to the family in a long time and everyone was welcome to join in their celebration of it.

Family and friends left the party in dribs and drabs. Nobody seemed as if they wanted to go home. It was one of those days that everyone wanted to last forever. Wilf had shown off a borrowed and almost new Dansette record player that kept everyone fully entertained. Songs like Love is a Many Splendoured Thing, Blue Suede Shoes, Rock around the Clock, Rose Marie and Stranger in Paradise were played and replayed. Since the end of wartime rationing in 1954 the country had developed an insatiable appetite for fun and good music and was determined to enjoy both without measure. Although the artists on the Embassy label of records, bought from the local Woolworth's store, could not compare to the original sounds of the Kings of RocknRoll it did not detract from the level of entertainment especially since Wilf had begged to borrow enough Embassy compilations from The King and I, Oklahoma and Carousel to last them well into the night.   At one point during the afternoon he picked up and placed his almost six-year-old daughter, Vivien, onto his size eights shoes and danced her around the room. 'He would teach her to dance', he thought. They did the Waltz, Jive, Quickstep, Rocknroll and even the Jitterbug. In his wildest dreams Wilf had never imagined he could ever have felt so happy. He did not deserve it.

After all the fun and laughter subsided and his home returned to being as quiet and as still as any house could possibly be with three young children Wilf walked upstairs and went into the front bedroom where his newly baptised bairn lay fast asleep. He stood silently, lost in the awe of the moment, before he stretched out his hand to touch his son's mass of blonde curly hair. "Kenneth, this is Kenneth, my son", he whispered before softly singing the song made famous by Harry Lauder:

Did you think I would leave you dying
When there's room on my horse for two
Climb up here Ken, we'll soon be flying
Back to the ranks so blue
Can you feel Ken I'm all a tremble
Perhaps it's the battle's noise
But I think it's that I remember
When we were two little boys.

This Kenneth would be safe. Nothing would happen to him. He wouldn't let it. He wouldn't be making another mistake. You could bet your bottom dollar on that.

CHAPTER TEN - A MIXED MOVE

Brenda and Wilf experienced the joy of having two more boys, Paul and Mark and another girl, Alma so named after Wilf's sister. Three of each, in total six. Wilf's children were his pride and joy and there was nothing he would not have done for any of them. He would have stood in their shoes and defended them with his life as he protected them with a passion fuelled by the fear of their loss. If any bugger dared to tread on their toes or threaten them in any way then they had better be ready for a fight because fight for them he would. He did not think them beyond reproach or that at times they did not warrant correction. He knew they were not saints and if accused of 'owt' he would always seek for the truth of the situation first and listen to his child's response before jumping the gun and passing a wrong judgement. He always delved into the facts of the matter and, if one of them proved to be in the wrong, then they were corrected and, if necessary, punished. Not punished by a hit, a slap or a good hiding as he had been but by being sent to bed without any tea or supper until apologies had been made and accepted all round.

At the start of the 'swinging sixties' the two-bedroom council house with its mature corner garden was bursting at the seams with children. They had taken possession of every square foot and inch of the house and, when other equally noisy children visited to play, children were like ants, everywhere. The large front bedroom was divided, in a fashion, into two halves and yet remained, at best, overcrowded. They would have to move house soon as they were unable to manage with the sleeping arrangements for very much longer. When an empty, but derelict, three bedroom terraced house came up for sale in the very street where Wilf had grown up, he was tempted to buy it. A closing order had however already been placed on the property because it was classified as unfit for human habitation and it would only be a matter of time before the council decided to demolish it altogether. At that time, an average house cost around £2,500 and although a terrace in Golden Hill could have been purchased for much less Wilf had no chance whatsoever of saving enough money for a deposit to buy one. His weekly wage was condemned and spent almost before it had been earned and most weeks he had no choice other than to ask for a 'sub' from one of his family members to tide him over until the next payday. Nationally, one in seven properties still had an outside toilet. Bill and Nell, although living in a different house, still lived in the same street they had lived in since before Kenneth's death. Terrence had recently married by special licence because his bride's parents had refused to give their consent to their union and also lived halfway down the same street. Alma, and her husband Alan lived a stone's throw away in the next street. Only young Bill had spread his wings to fly a massive five miles away when he married a girl who, according to the local gossip brigade, seemed a cut and a half above the rest. The mix-match was a talking point for weeks on the corner of the High Street. 'Oil and water dunna mix' the bevy of buxom beauties solidly agreed. 'He'd be back wome (home) with his tail between his legs before he had chance to put his feet under the bloody kitchen table. Just you mark my words' the ringleader declared. 'Any bugger could have told the daft sod that much. You could tack a lad outta the slums but you'd never tack the slums outta the lad. No amount of dressing up in posh clothes would alter that. No, he'd be back. Nothing so bloody sure' was the united opinion of the tittle-tattle contingent.

Like a homing pigeon and akin to so many others who were born and bred on the Hill, Wilf was programmed to return to the familiarity of his roots and the compelling terraces of close-knit community life. Only one small thing stood in his way. The unfit for habitation house had a price tag of twenty pounds on it and Wilf hadn't got twenty pennies in his back pocket let alone twenty pounds. Unbeknown to Wilf the family held a meeting where it was unanimously agreed to pass a cap round. Every one put in what they could afford and more to help him out. Quite amazingly, they managed to raise the money and Wilf bought a house in exchange for a twenty-pound note.

The house had no gas, electricity or running water connected to it and was really just a shell, a hovel, but

Wilf relished the challenge it presented. There was no money to pay builders and the like. All the extensive works were done entirely by family and the majority of it by Wilf's own hands. Every window was removed and replaced. Floors were dug up, dug out and replaced with concrete ones. The roof was repaired and all the tiles replaced. At least, one room was decorated with odd rolls of wallpaper, donated leftovers from various family and friends. Different colours from more than half-empty cans of paint were mixed together to create the most bizarre colours that were duly daubed onto the new doors and lintels. Beggars could definitely not be choosers. The building inspector, complete with his monocle and clipboard, visited regularly. He monitored, approved, or recommended further improvements to the never-ending work in progress. Every night and every weekend Wilf, Brenda and family members worked around-the-clock to build a home fit for their precious family to live in. It turned out to be something akin to watching a community of Amish working together non-stop in order to build a brother's barn. Occasions when everyone dug deep, pulled together, worked together, ate and laughed together to get the job done. On more than one occasion Wilf silently feared he had bitten off more than he could chew but he never voiced his doubts. He worked from dusk till dawn whenever time allowed and slowly but surely the restoration was complete and the building inspector's final visit was imminent. On his visit everyone, including the dog Judy, held their breath for all they were worth. The Health Inspector had the power to say 'yea' or 'nay' to the provisionally completed works.

The closing order had to be rescinded and the house approved for human habitation before anyone would be allowed to live in it. The building inspector, with a nod of his head and the wriest of smiles plastered across his normally expressionless face, gave the house his official stamp of approval. With shouts of jubilation ringing in his ears Wilf felt 'chuffed to bits'. Although he had worked his fingers almost to the bone he had succeeded in building a home for his family and one approved by the bloody building inspector himself. It had been a mammoth task and one that he would never be tempted to face again unless, of course, he was given little or no choice in the matter. It was a long hard slog but he had done it and a completion date was agreed.

The night before the move and just as dusk started to fall, Wilf decided to visit the house alone. He felt pleased with himself and wanted to savour the occasion. He slowly and deliberately walked through the ground floor. All of the rooms were unrecognisable. What an achievement. He walked up the extremely narrow steep staircase and into the front bedroom. He stood motionless as the new owner of the house on the corner and looked through the bedroom window straight across the road at the front door of the house he lived in as a boy with his brother Kenneth. He peered up and down the street, totally mesmerised and stared until the electric lights melted away and slowly reappeared as the dimmest of gas lamps. He watched intently as the street filled with his playmates from years before. He watched them toying together without, it seemed, an apparent care in the world. He was stuck to them like glue as they laughed at stupid jokes whilst kicking a ball loudly on the end of a wall before running around as if their backsides were on fire in games of Tick and Blind Man's Bluff. Shouts of 'You're out' and denials of the fact filled the air. Just as Wilf was about to smile at his reminiscent childhood scenes the surreal frame froze at exactly the same second as he saw him. He gasped, as his eyes met those of his brother, Kenneth. He was as clear as day to him. His back and shoulders rested on the wall outside the house where they used to live with one leg crossed over the top of the other. He looked exactly the same as Wilf remembered him. He had not changed at all and was even dressed in the same old play clothes with a cloth cap on top of his head. Wilf wanted to run to him and tell him he was sorry. He wanted to embrace him, laugh with him, tell him how much he loved him and had missed him, but he blinked and he was gone. In the twinkling of an eye he had disappeared. Wilf tried his best to visualise him again. He concentrated, focused his gaze, willing him to reappear, but he had vanished. Perhaps, because he had returned, like an Australian boomerang, to live again in the most fateful of streets, with the saddest of memories, he might catch sight of his brother again within the shadows of the street's past. He hoped so. He really hoped so.

That the house did not have an inside toilet, bath or garden did not seem significant at the time of the move, but proved to be very significant indeed. Six children constantly running down the backyard to use the toilet was a nightmare in itself, particularly during the winter months when a paraffin lamp hung on the stop tap to prevent the toilet from freezing up. Sheets of newspaper, stuck crudely on a nail on the back of the toilet door and used as tissue paper, were always damp yet were minor discomforts when compared to the filling of the tin bath for a weekly scrub. The boys, who did paper-rounds to help out with the family income, spotted a real bath discarded on wasteland and brought it home on the back of trolleys they had made from two sets of old pram wheels. The bath took pride of place in the small kitchen but was never unfortunately plumbed in. This did not however prevent it from being regularly utilised. By using saucepans, it was manually filled and emptied whenever someone wanted a bath. Many a bath was taken in the small cramped kitchen surrounded by dirty dishes, saucepans and the smell of White Windsor washing soap. It saved a lot of time, money and effort to occasionally put the young boys in the bath together. They obviously enjoyed this practicality not least because they created a fun time from the experience. They regularly, and quite disgustingly in the girls' minds, held trumping competitions. They crudely judged the winner by the amount of bubbles the gusts of wind created in the water. Although an overall winner was never unanimously agreed on, shouts of 'that was the best yet, come on admit it' mixed with the sounds and splashes of water and laughter were endured or enjoyed, depending on the perspective of the other family members. It was impossible not to hear the goings-on from the other side of the curtain that separated the kitchen from the middle room. Bath times were not however always fun and games. In fact none of the children enjoyed sharing the kitchen come bathroom with dead animals. Many a bath was taken by a solitary child as they scarily stared into the deep black eyes of a dead rabbit hanging by its back legs from a nail on the back of the kitchen door. When not in use the bath was covered over with an old internal door and doubled-up as a low-level worktop in order to dish out all manner of delicacies including rabbit stew, cow's heart and stuffing, potato pie with not much meat in it or the favourite 'dish of day' liver and onions.

An alternative use was also being found for the old tin bath that had been re-housed on the wall in the backyard. It had quickly undergone an amazing transformation to become a trough for plucking and gutting dead chickens in. The children were all informed not to get too attached to the cute cuddly chicks reared in the hearth of the fireplace and, on no account, to give them names because if they didn't prove to be good layers then they'd make jolly good roasters. Many a mouthful of chicken breast got stuck on the way down especially if a new brood of chicks were cheerfully chirping in the hearth while the family ate a Sunday roast chicken dinner. Egg shells were dried out in the oven and crushed while vegetable peelings were boiled in saucepans before being mixed together to feed the hens.

Anything discarded that the boys thought useful they 'delivered' on their trolleys to the house including, on one occasion, a brown leather seat from the front compartment of an old Ford van. It took pride of place as an unusual easy chair in the middle room. In many ways the house lacked the warmth and facilities of the council property they had left behind and this was especially noticeable during the long winter months. The net curtains so proudly displayed on every window of the house regularly froze to the inside of the glass during the coldest of nights. It proved a job and a half to pull them off the glass without tearing them. At first the children argued about who would get to tug the nets free. Jack Frost had so successfully frozen them that they looked like an integral part of his own unique spiky spidery patterns. But the novelty of the game soon wore off and sometimes the nets remained frozen to the windows all day and night.

At other times of the year the children missed the garden and especially the swing. They were not alone in their feelings of loss and readjustment. Wilf missed his garden so much so that he took possession of an allotment, complete with the new experience and joy of his very own greenhouse. He produced the most delicious of vegetables and the most beautiful of chrysanthemums. The quality of his produce was so outstanding that cabbages and carrots regularly went missing from his plot. He quickly realised that some cheeky bugger was thieving off him and although he could believe it he hated the thought of it. He would rather give his proud produce away than have it stolen from him. It was as if an unspoken divine principle was being broken right under his very nose so he decided to take drastic steps in an attempt to catch the poachers red handed. Late into the evening, on more than one night, he donned his thickest coat, filled a flask with tea, left the house and camped out in his greenhouse for as long as it took to catch the blighters. He never revealed to anyone who he had caught red-handed with their hands in the cookie jar but suffice to say that they never returned to do it again. Wilf's garden produce was so wholesome that the owner of the local corner shop offered to buy as much lettuce, radish, cucumber, carrots, cabbage, spring onions and anything else he could grow. At first the offer, handed to him on plate, seemed a real blessing, until the owner suggested, that in return for her generosity his eldest wench might work alongside her in the shop every day after school and all day on Saturdays. After weeks of training and in an attempt to boost the family income the owner offered to pay his wench seven shillings and sixpence (thirty-seven and a half pence in decimal currency) a week in addition to giving her as much knocked fruit as she could carry home with her. It was an unexpected bonus and Brenda quickly cut away the mould from the redeemed fruit declaring it fit for consumption by her ever-hungry family. Wilf's wench took to the little job like a duck to water. She thoroughly enjoyed serving customers and reckoning up their bills using a pencil on the marble slab that formed the counter. She soaked up her experiences of customer care like a sponge and the owner assured her that she had the makings of a very good shop-keeper.

The terrace undoubtedly had some advantages, not least the fact that it had another bedroom and no rent had to be scraped together on a regular weekly basis for its occupancy. The independence of owning something of their own outweighed the loss of the amenities of a council property. However, when this opinion resulted in the emptying of chamber pots and carrying buckets of slops down the stairs, through the house and out to the toilet at the bottom of the yard to be emptied, the concept of home-ownership grandeur dissipated in the stark light of reality. Electricity sockets were also in short supply. None had been installed in the front room or any of the bedrooms encouraging more than a degree of creativity. During the sixties the majority of homes owned record players and Wilf's was no exception. The family loved music but in order to play records in the parlour a special type of socket was needed that enabled the record player to be connected to the electricity supply in the ceiling in place of the light bulb. This was a wonderful improvisation during day light hours but proved difficult as night fell because both the light and the record player could not be connected to the electricity supply at the same time. It therefore proved an immense advantage to have a streetlight positioned just outside the house. If all else failed then the family could dance in the street, under the light of the lamppost to the sound of the sixties playing in their ears from a record player connected to the light socket in the front room! They were often frowned upon for such a public demonstration of common and mawkish behaviour. Such revelry however did not happen too often and was reserved for the most special of occasions. Celebrations were thoroughly enjoyed by all including every bugger in the street who had often been left with no alternative other than to join in the fun.

Late in 1969 Parlophone released a record that became a top ten hit for The Hollies. The words of the song, written by America's Scott and Russell, were inspired by the story of 'Boys Town' and the film of the same name starring Spencer Tracey. Its lyrics touched every chord of Wilf's heart and he more than struggled to listen to it. Due to its popularity however the words seemed to ring out from every radio station and house in the country for weeks. It was almost impossible not to hear:

'The road is long, With many a winding turn
That leads us to who knows where, Who knows where?
But I'm strong, Strong enough to carry him,
He ain't heavy, he's my brother.
So on we go. His welfare is my concern...'

Whenever Wilf heard the song he immediately turned the radio or the television off and even those closest to him did not really understand why. In truth, it did not take much working out. The words obviously reminded him of his brother Kenneth. As boys Kenneth had never been too heavy for him. Wilf had lifted him up a dozen times or more a day to reach an apple off a tree or to play Piggie Back Rides and his physical weight had never felt heavy to him; not once. Wilf was strong enough to carry his brother anywhere and everywhere. Since his death however he had carried him albeit in a very different way every day of his life like a huge anchor hooked into the depths of his heart. He did not need to hear the words of a pop song to remind him that his brother's welfare was and would always be his concern and, in this respect, he had failed him and his failure had resulted in his death. The weight of responsibility for his tragic loss proved, for a lifetime, to be infinitely heavier to bear than the literal weight of his brother had ever been.

Wilf's family grew up overnight and one day he was faced with the reality of the fact that he did not own them. They did not belong to him and they would not live under his roof forever. They would all soon stand on their own two feet and face the world and whatever it held for them head on. He worried that they would be hurt. That friends and husbands and wives would not respect and love his children as much as he had and still did. Not surprisingly then he found it extremely difficult to think of them flying the nest and the security he had done everything in his power to ensure it afforded them. This proved especially true with his first-born who, at only nineteen had told him that she wanted to get married. To say that he wrestled long and hard with the request was an understatement. Although his Brenda had only been eighteen when he had wed her, a Father's perspective on marriage was very different indeed. He bucked at being expected to feel proud to do his duty and give his too-young-to-be-married daughter away. He wondered if anyone had stopped to think what it would mean to him to submit to her request. His daughter would change her surname from Hackney to Jones. He would no longer be recorded as her next of kin, his shoulder to rely on. He accepted that sooner or later he would have to part with the only 'things' he truly cherished in life, his children. And yet, on balance, he understood that it was the natural order and motion of life and even if he had wanted to he would not have been able to put the brakes on or change its course. So, with as much of his heart as he could, he agreed to give her away and chose to do so with his blessing.

Clothes were purchased from Great Universal Stores, a catalogue mail order firm. It took weeks of ordering, trying on, parcelling up and sending back, until eventually everyone had an outfit. As Wilf stood back and looked at his firstborn and the rest of his children all shooting up around him he experienced the reality of the words sung by Topol playing Tevye and Norma Crane as Golde in Fiddler on the Roof:

Is this the little girl I carried?
Is this the little boy at play?
I don't remember growing older.
When did they?
When did she get to be a beauty?
When did he grow to be so tall?
Wasn't it yesterday, that they were small?
Seedlings turn overnight to sunflowers,
Blossoming even as we gaze.

What eased the first blow was the wisdom and knowledge that freedom and trust were two of the most gracious gifts afforded to children by their parents and, invariably, children carried the love of their family with them however many miles away from home they travelled. After all was said and done, there was no love, not even that of the most devoted partner that could compare to the unselfish love of a Father who reflected the true meaning of the word. A Father who was and would always be an all-weather friend and one who could be relied upon to give his all for those he loved without any hope or expectation of recompense.

As his family grew Wilf hoped that his six children would each have six children of their own enabling him to have and spoil thirty-six grandchildren! He called this a quiver full. A quiver, in this sense, is a leather pouch used to safely hold arrows and that's what his children were to him. Six of the very best arrows and ones that he would shoot as straight and as far and as high into the sky as he possibly could. Hopefully, if he had anything to do with it, he would shoot them into a life filled with health, happiness, love and success. Wilf was always at his happiest with a babe to hold, bless and cradle in his strong arms. He became his children's, his grandchildren's and his great-grandchildren's quiver. Their shield, protector and defender whether they wanted it or not and woe betide any bugger who attempted to threaten, damage, blunt or break any of his arrows.

One of Wilf's simplest and most enjoyable pleasures in life came about as a result of feeding and studying his garden birds. He watched them build their nests and fledge their young. It was difficult to do this however without his thoughts not turning to his brother's talented sketches of birds of every description. How he wished he had been allowed to save just one of his etchings but they had all disappeared soon after his death. He even wondered if Miss Jardine his teacher had saved the picture she had put up on her kitchen wall all those years before as a memento and in remembrance of a blonde curly haired boy who had a special gift and talent for art. There was and would always be an empty place, an empty chair at every significant family occasion tingeing celebrations with sadness and an overwhelming longing for his lost brother.

As his allotment became too big to manage Wilf settled for a smaller garden patch just outside his flat and decked it out with the brightest and best of flowers, including forget-me-nots, which he planted underneath the biggest buddleia in the area and which, in turn, attracted butterflies of every description. His great grandchildren regularly watched on as Wilf tended the buddleia and told them a story of two very special caterpillars.

"One day in a garden far away in a land called the Rising Sun lived two caterpillar friends named Sunrise and Sunset. Sunrise was far more advanced in every way than Sunset having been born a good two weeks earlier. Both caterpillars, like all caterpillars, were always hungry and ate their way through lots and lots of greenery. They grew so big that they both ended up bursting out of their overcoats. Fortunately they both had another layer on underneath so this did not bother them too much. Sunrise held the record for bursting out of her coat because she had done it four times already. They both found this very funny indeed as they rolled around and laughed together in the summer sunshine. Despite their compulsive eating habits they always found time to talk to each other. Their world seemed very big indeed in fact so big that the thought of it sometimes blew their tiny minds away. It was also a world full of danger. Sometimes they would hide together trembling on the underside of leaves in fear of being seen and thrown off the plants by one of the giant's huge hands or, even worse, being eaten alive by one of the monsters with a massive beak. At night when the world slept and the moths came out to play they talked together about their futures.

"We will always be friends, won't we?" asked Sunset. "Most definitely" Sunrise replied. "Nothing will separate us. Together forever, that's us."

"You won't leave me then?" questioned Sunset. "Leave you. I will never leave you. Where would I go? This is our world. We belong here. It has everything we need. No, I will never leave you. Never", Sunrise replied.

The very next day Sunrise went missing. Sunset searched all over their familiar garden patch looking high and low for her friend but she could not find her anywhere and hoped nothing awful had happened to her. Two weeks went by very quickly but Sunset never gave up hope of seeing her friend again. She always felt ravenous and had eaten so much food that she had burst out of her overcoat twice and felt big enough to burst right out of it again. She was so full that she decided to settle down for a mid-day nap on a beautiful buddleia in the friendly giant's garden patch.

"Sunset, It's me. Look at me. I can fly. The world is massive. It is so much bigger than we ever dreamt it could ever be. I have been transformed and it's wonderful", yelled Sunrise as she flew over the buddleia and patch of garden that she used to think was the big wide world. "It's me. It's me, Sunset, look up" she called but Sunset could not hear her. She was far too focused on her own world and unable to tune in to what was a very different frequency indeed. So, Sunset settled back down for a long nap not knowing the transformation that awaited her too.

"Granddad is that a true story?" asked Wilf's youngest great grandchild. "In a way, it is" he wisely replied.

Wilf celebrated his 70th birthday with family and friends and enjoyed every minute of it. He indulged himself in some of his favourite music especially from the worlds of film and theatre. He loved The Student Prince starring Mario Lanza; If I Was A Rich Man sung by Topol in Fiddler on the Roof; One Fine Day from Madame Butterfly, especially the English rendition by Joan Hammond, What a Wonderful World by Louis Armstrong, Climb Every Mountain from the Sound of Music and last, but by no means least, Goodbye from the White Horse Inn by Joseph Locke. He also had his very own von Tramp, as opposed to von Trapp family, who regularly performed their own renditions of all kinds of sounds of music.

Wilf had not told anyone however that he had been experiencing shortness of breath, on exertion, for quite some time. He had visited the doctor several times and after numerous blood tests was treated with iron tablets for anaemia. Unfortunately, this treatment did not rectify the problem and after attending an appointment with the practice nurse, whom he playfully called Gladys Emmanuel (after a nurse in Open All Hours, the TV sitcom starring Ronnie Barker) she spoke to the GP regarding her concerns about his blood test results. Wilf walked out of the GP Surgery holding a letter to take with him that very night to the Medical Assessment Unit at the local hospital. On his return home from the surgery he did not mention his concerns to Brenda but rather carefully dialled his eldest wench's telephone number. He held the receiver close to his ear as he heard it rhythmically ring out. 'It was teatime and she would probably be busy. Just in from working at the local college' he thought as it continued to ring. He regularly said that he was proud of all his children, including his eldest wench who was a Lecturer. His wench a lecturer! So much for washing, ironing, cooking and cleaning! The phone continued to ring.

CHAPTER ELEVEN –

A REVERSAL OF ROLES

JANUARY 2002

"Can you get the phone? Can somebody please get the phone" Wilf's daughter shouted. She rushed towards it and managed to grab the receiver before it stopped ringing.

"Hi Dad" she responded in surprise. Her Father never telephoned her at dinnertime. On this occasion however his call could not have waited. He needed her right then and there and roles and responsibilities were set to turn an almost full circle.

Does his wench wish that she hadn't reached the phone in time and, in desperation, her Father had telephoned another one of his children? If so then this book would never have been written and the tears and the truth contained within its pages would have remained buried forever.

As it was it was meant to be.

***

That night in late January 2002 his eldest wench and his youngest son accompanied their Father to the local Medical Assessment Unit at the City General Hospital. As a result of preliminary tests, Wilf was admitted and underwent further investigations including a bone marrow test which involved extracting marrow from his thighbone under local anaesthetic.

On a painful day in February 2002 Wilf's eldest wench and his youngest son sat alongside their Father while the Consultant, with specialist nurse alongside, sensitively explained to them that their Father had a terminal condition known as multiple myeloma. In plain language multiple myeloma is cancer of the bone marrow.

The shock felt almost overwhelming, like being hit by a ten-ton lorry in a head-on collision. The family's familiar world, their security was rocked, unexpectedly shaken to its very foundations. 'How could their Father, their Dad, their Granddad, have been issued with such a stark unbelievable death sentence? Wilf was the strongest man in the world, wasn't he? He had always fought his family's corners and stood up for them all even when they may not have deserved or expected it. He had believed in them when nobody else gave a damn and would have given every one of them his last pound in his pocket. No, he could not possibly have been so ill he would die and leave them, could he?' thoughts and scenarios overwhelmed them.

'Why was the sun still shining on a frosty morning in a bright blue sky?' they silently questioned in their own individual ways. 'Had it not heard their news? How dare it shine?' they felt swamped, angry and completely bewildered as leaflets, information, telephone numbers and appointment cards flew at them from every direction.

Their combined fight for life had started and Wilf would fight cancer in the same way as he had fought everything else in his life, with courage, dignity and resolve.

In an instant, shut in a small room with a Consultant Haematologist and a serious specialist nurse, their world was irrevocably changed as they reluctantly and tentatively started their journey with the big C. Life was never going to be quite the same ever again.

Wilf, Brenda and his little brood fought many rounds in the boxing ring against the giant of cancer. Sometimes they found themselves struggling 'on the ropes' as if tangled in a sticky web of fear and despair. Other times they would feel they had delivered a fatal blow to the big C as the enemy hit the floor in the light of encouraging treatment reports. The giant however was only ever knocked down and never truly knocked out. The family were undoubtedly weakened and sometimes felt as if their legs would give way underneath them as the awful ogre stood to its feet, lifted its gruesome gloves and prepared for the next round in a fight that, with the best will, stamina and positive thinking in the world, they could never have won.

Wilf received over 200 units of blood in just over two years supported by appointments with the Consultant specialist at least every three weeks. Cancer took slow possession of his body but his mind and spirit were not for sale and were never relinquished.

Since the birth of his son Kenneth in 1956 Wilf celebrated a part of Christmas Day with his lad and his family and friends at the local workingmen's club, but the Christmas of 2003 found him lying in a hospital bed. He had attended the clinic on Christmas Eve and discovered he needed an urgent blood transfusion. Without further ado, family plans for Christmas Day were cancelled in favour of sitting beside him on the saddest and loneliest of wards. In spite of the most stalwart of efforts to create an upbeat and pleasant atmosphere it was obvious that no nurse, nor doctor for that matter, really wanted to be on duty on Christmas Day. All the NHS Christmas hats, crackers, chocolates and even the cheerless dimly lit tree positioned in the corner of the ward did not convince the patients and visitors otherwise. Only the poorliest patients were in hospital on 25th December that year and sadly Wilf was one of them.

As his eldest wench sat beside him watching the now familiar drips of blood feed into his veins and restore some colour to her Father's ashen body their relationship, which had deepened over recent months, took on a very different dimension. The only way to describe what happened between them is to liken it to a mighty and magnificent oak tree. Below the beauty of the oak's branches, filled with leaves and acorns and cradled by the strongest and sturdiest of trunks, lays the roots, the anchor of the tree itself. Roots that tunnel far under the cold earth, deep down under the surface and bring life and sustenance to the body of the tree, holding it steady during the many storms it weathers throughout its long life. Because of the heart wrenching challenges he had been forced to face in his battle for life the roots of Wilf's relationships forced their way through deep and painful ground before unexpectedly reaping a harvest of richness and beauty beyond compare. Ties and bonds deepened through the most awful of tribulations and created a trust and a levelling of positions that in the usual mundane run of life may never have evolved and matured. At times and particularly whilst sitting in hospital wards, they appeared almost as equals, as friends, not solely as a Father and his Daughter. The hours spent together in clinics, wards, and even preparing a funeral plan reinforced their love, understanding and respect for each other and reshaped their relationship into a bond that became deeper than life itself. Perhaps a bond similar to the one Wilf had known with the brother he had lost. A bond sensitive enough to hold, cherish and value dreams yet proved strong enough to withstand the most awful of truths. The playing field of life became smoother as Wilf reminded his wench that death, often referred to as the great leveller, was in itself an equaliser. He further underlined this belief by firmly reminding her that 'No bugger brings anythin' into the world with 'em when they're born and no bugger, however grand and mighty, takes anything out with 'em when they leave it'.

True to form, Wilf could not wait to get his backside out of hospital and in the early hours of Boxing Day 2003 after pestering staff for an early discharge his eldest wench brought her Father home. He had been robbed of his usual Christmas Day and while he had life in his body and breath in his lungs he would celebrate it even if it meant doing so a day late. After a couple of hours' rest Wilf insisted on visiting the club for a drink with his son and family. Perhaps he knew that this would be his last Christmas and his final chance to celebrate the birth of his son and the meaning of Christmas in his usual manner and custom. So he settled for a Boxing Day celebration of Christmas Day and what's more, the date on the calendar did not matter one iota. Boxing Day became Christmas Day to him and those he loved. With all the strength he could generate he got himself suited and booted, ready to do his family proud and create a memory that they would all never forget. Suit, shirt, tie, complete with tie pin of course and shoes blacked 'n polished 'til he could see his face shine in 'em. It was fun all round in the lounge bar of the club and if he felt as if he was knocking on death's door he did not show it and his Fatherly façade remained intact.

After Christmas Wilf's days of reasonable health became fewer and yet he remained good humoured and generous hearted. He even offered, much to the dismay of his children, to donate his body to medical science/research if it would help to save the lives of other people. The Consultant insisted that he had done more than enough for research not least by the positive and strong manner in which he handled his illness. He had also agreed to take part in a trial of the drug Thalidomide in the treatment of multiple myeloma and in so doing helped to provide important evidence of its efficacy.

Wilf saw and enjoyed the Spring. He delighted to see the appearance of snowdrops and crocus and became desperate to make the birth of two more of his great-grandchildren. One was due in April and the other one at the end of May. He could not wait to hold them in his arms and bless them. He had a wide range of friends from an even wider spectrum of backgrounds and from all walks of life. He was a people person who could talk to anyone about almost anything. He particularly valued a friend name Jack, a wonderful Jewish man who spoke openly to him of his faith in God. Wilf shared with him his broad views and opinions on faith and, from the depth of their friendship and mutual respect of each other's stance, their hands and hearts joined across the gulf between the old and new testaments of the bible. As a result of his Jewish friendship one of Wilf's favourite words became: 'Shalom', a Hebrew word meaning a complete sense of peace. He learned and appreciated from Jack that Hebrew words go beyond their spoken pronunciation and convey both feeling and emotion. Shalom, as he came to understand it, relayed a feeling of contentment, completeness, wholeness, well-being and harmony and whenever a person left Wilf throughout the latter years of his life his parting word to them would often be Shalom; the blessing and peace of God be with you and upon you and those you love. He often followed this with a more traditional Good night and God bless; an adage given for good measure.

During the latter part of his illness Wilf began to reminisce about his brother Kenneth and one night while his eldest wench sat alongside him he started to tell her his account of the death of his brother. The saying that the 'truth will set you free' was that night tested to the hilt as the hands of time turned back the clock to the fateful summer's day in July 1941 and the most painful of memories were exposed and relived.

CHAPTER TWELVE –
THE TRUTH OR A LIE

Wilf woke early to a beautiful sunny Sunday morning. His brother Bill was at the bottom of the big double bed in the front bedroom of the home of Mr and Mrs Williams underneath the finest of sheets and blankets that he'd ever seen. Wilf had not slept very much having tossed and turned the night away as he relived the events of the previous day over and over in his troubled mind. Fear tightened her grip of him and he was unable to shake her off during the longest and most accusing of nights.

Mrs Williams raided her own pantry and started to cook a full week's ration of bacon and real eggs for all three of the young 'ens but Wilf came downstairs with no stomach for food. Not long after he had counted the grandfather clock strike midnight in the parlour under the bedroom where they lay, he heard the most blood-curdling scream imaginable reverberate into the darkness of the night only to rebound and echo into the depths of his own young heart. He could have sworn, on oath, that the screams came from the top of the street near to his house, the second one in from the corner of the road.

151

Wilf remembered thinking that it sounded like a trapped animal, perhaps a fox, as it howled out its pain into the darkness of night. And yet, he also reasoned that it might have been the shrill cry of a woman giving birth, so piercing was the sound of its pain and pitch.

Fortunately, the warmth of the morning sun and the smell of bacon and eggs proved more than enough to make his mouth water with anticipation of a feast. He therefore quickly concluded that his recollections were part of a dream or a nightmare. 'Yes, that's what it was' he silently declared. 'It had just been a nightmare on the heels of a fitful dream about Kenneth. A dream in which he had seen his brother laughing his mismatched socks off over the prank he had managed to pull off on his top-notch big brother.' And so, sitting around the table, complete with cloth and condiments, Wilf started to wolf-down the bacon, real eggs and dollops of sauce.

Hardly stopping for a breath and with food bursting out of both sides of his overfull mouth he looked into the wide eyes of his two younger siblings and said: "He'll be home today. Don't ya worry about it. He'll be home today and I'll give him what for I will, for tryin' to pull a fast 'en off on me". Immediately followed by:

"Can we save some of this for our Kenneth please? Or else he'll never believe me when I tell him what we've got down our necks for breakfast" looking imploringly at Mrs Williams.

"There's plenty more where that came from" she responded positively but all the time thinking that she'd never seen plates of food disappear quite so quickly in all her life. Her half-a-smile expression however belied a depth of apprehension and fear that she did not dare put a name or voice to. Silently, as she went into the small but well-equipped kitchen with her arms full of plates already wiped clean in a most impolite fashion she whispered her prayer:

"Dear God, let the worst of it not be true". Let them find the lad safe, alive and well". Mrs Williams, or Elsie, as she was commonly known by her neighbours, had been up since the crack of dawn while the house remained still and quiet warming milk for baby Terrence. She then took all the time in the world to wash and change the pleasant little chap. People around about her thought she had not wanted children of her own and some had even branded her a selfish cow for not having had them. The truth however could not have been farther away from their arrogant assumptions, judgements and sentencing. Elsie lived in the painful shadows of both longing and loss. She had in fact desperately wanted a bairn of her own but as the months raced by like clockwork she thought herself cursed and forever barren. She therefore relished, in the stillness of the early summer morning and shielded behind the security of black out curtains, the joy of bathing and feeding a bairn even though she knew, only too well, that he was only a borrowed babe. In the most extraordinary circumstances he had been loaned to her; the midwife's babe of all babes was under her roof and for an entire night she pretended that he was her very own.

Elsie had also been unable to sleep although the reason for her insomnia was nothing at all to do with Kenneth. She never doubted that the young boy would be found safe and well and so she stayed awake rocking and cradling Terrence for the entire night. She imagined and pretended what it would have been like to have nursed her own bairn. She had often seen Nell running backwards and forwards, up and down the streets delivering live and sadly sometimes dead bairns. Over time however she lost all hope that Nell would ever knock on her door to advise or help her with maternal matters. Yet a strange quirk of unexpected events, and an equally unexpected toss of the dice resulted in Nell's bairn being cherished by Elsie, the selfish cow whom it was widely assumed did not want any babes of her own. Contrary to popular opinion Elsie would, in reality, have given all the tea in China, all her own personal possessions, so envied by her judge and jury, for just one bairn, just one babe to love and call her own. How she longed to be accepted by the other predominately Catholic Mothers who stood chatting in the street and over low backyard walls that separated the warren of terraces. Her judge and jury had however discussed, decided and declared their narrow-minded 'Guilty' verdict without an apparent ounce of mercy or compassion. The judgement was quick and easy since none of her accusers could remember having seen her at Mass so, when it came down to procreation and pregnancy she was obviously not a good Catholic girl. On the inside of purgatory's prison Elsie had however very slowly resigned herself to the shameful fact that her womb was closed, perhaps cursed by God, and would never bear a babe. If the truth was known, she had stopped attending church services simply because she could no longer face the pretence of it. She left behind the good and faithful who lived in gregarious glass houses to throw their misplaced stones of accusation and condemnation. Elsie however had her own altar of sacrifice where she prayed and pleaded for a miracle every day that God sent and for one night she pretended that all her prayers had been answered as she rocked a borrowed babe to sleep.

By the time the bacon and eggs were on the table Terrence had dropped off to sleep outside in the morning sunshine tucked snugly in his drawer of a cot Elsie had relined with her own linen and her own crocheted blankets. She had been hard pressed to decide what to wrap him in and found it very difficult indeed to choose an outfit to dress her borrowed bairn in. In fact, she had been spoilt for choice. She had locked drawers full of knitted and crocheted blankets, shawls and outfits all secretly placed between sheets of carefully folded tissue paper, all waiting for the never-to-be babies that she had prayed and yearned for over so many disappointing months and years. Sometimes her 'visitor' would be late and her hopes would soar until the tell-tale dreaded cramps and stomach pains started. She would hold all the muscles below her waistline as tight as she possibly could. She would sit down, put up her feet and hardly take a breath as she prayed that her visitor would not arrive. But it always did. Elsie could surely then have been forgiven for being too pre-occupied, hidden away in the back bedroom, watching her very own make believe babe sleep to have heard the pandemonium and pantomime that unfolded late into the night in the very street where she lived.

Wilf had rallied in the glow of a breakfast that was fit for the King of England. He cheered himself with thoughts of seeing Kenneth and even tentatively planned, although subconsciously, one of the best days out for them in his almost twelve yet going on twenty-one heart and mind. 'Yes', he reassured himself again. 'It had been a nightmare of the worst possible kind. That's all it had been. Hadn't it?' he reasoned.

His optimism and daydreaming was brought to an abrupt end by a stern rapping on the Williams's front door. Muffled sounds ensued, but try as he may, Wilf, and no bugger else for that matter, including Mrs Williams whose ear was pressed butt up to the middle door, could possibly hear a word of what was being said. Everyone did however hear the front door softly close and the middle door that separated the two rooms gently open.

It felt like an age had passed during the time it took Mr Williams to come back into the room but one glance at the look on his face was enough to turn Wilf's stomach. The bacon and eggs threatened to find their way back up as Fear turned him into jelly in a split second of time. She engulfed him. Swamped him. Threatened to stifle and suffocate every ounce of life out of him as Her presence filled the Williams's house.

Archie did not stop to look at the children. In fact he deliberately averted his gaze as, with his head lowered and with a white envelope clutched in his left hand he walked slowly and deliberately towards Elsie. He placed his right arm around her shoulder and whispered something inaudible to the rest of the room into her left ear. Elsie's reaction became both instinctive and instantaneous. Her left hand went straight up and covered her mouth as if to prevent it from gasping and spilling out the horror of what she had heard in front of the children. With an air of composure Archie led Elsie into the kitchen and closed the door behind them.

Bravado and Dutch courage combined together and tried to overcome the blood curdling Fear that had taken possession of Wilf's young body and mind. He stiffened up and looked straight at Alma and Billy, who were both completely oblivious to the seriousness of the situation, and with half a laugh he blurted out: "It's nowt to do with our Kenneth, Dunna worry. It's nowt to do with him."

In spite of his unfounded demonstration of bold conviction Fear froze him solid to the spot as he watched intently as the door handle from the kitchen to the middle room slowly turned and Mr and Mrs Williams came back into the room together.

Elsie entered the room first holding Terrence firmly in front of her. He was dressed in the finest array of baby clothes any bugger in the vicinity would ever have seen. For some unknown reason Wilf wanted to jump up and snatch him from her arms. He wanted to grab his baby

157

brother to have something belonging to him to hold onto but instead he remained glued to the spot.

"Let's all go into the parlour" Elsie said. "Mr Williams needs to speak to you all and it's nice and sunny in there."

Everything was running in slow motion. Words of encouragement and direction seemed to float around the room and hang in muffled limbo in the tense, oxygen-starved aura that had invaded their space and time. The three children were nudged and shuffled into the front room together.

The sun did light up the room. Mrs Williams was right about that much but nothing in the room seemed tangible to any of them and especially to Wilf. The children found themselves huddled together on a two-seater best brocade settee facing a black-lead grate that looked as if it had never seen a speck of dust or dirt since its manufacture. 'Perhaps it was just for show an' a fire had never even been lit in it' Wilf pondered. The arms of the settee were hidden with cream lace covers that immediately attracted Alma's attention as she started to closely inspect them. She turned them over and over as they distracted her focus from what was happening around about her. A most uncomfortable silence filled the room.

'What was it? What was happening?' Wilf thought but did not find his voice to ask the question; it had been paralysed together with the rest of his body. From the corner of the immaculate room Fear herself firmly crossed her arms in front of her black clothed super slim body as with the sickliest of smirks she engulfed the room's occupants overriding every other ounce of sense and feeling.

Mrs Williams sat down on one of the armchairs positioned closest to the settee cradling and gently patting Terrence. Wilf was sitting in the middle of the settee, Alma to the right of him and young Bill on his left. Just when he thought the room would explode with tension Mr Williams stooped down low in front of them and with solemnity and a perfunctory tone of voice said, as gently as he possibly could:

"I am sorry to tell you that you will not be seeing your brother Kenneth again. He has gone to be with God, in heaven".

"Liar" Wilf screamed as he jumped to his feet and pointed his finger into the face of Mr Williams. "You're a bloody liar" he repeated, as shock and disbelief welled-up within him and vehemently declared the unbelievable truth to be a lie. And yet, all the time in the very depth of his almost twelve but going on twenty-one-year old heart he knew that this man, this kind man's words were, in fact, the most awful truth. His brother, his confidant and his friend must be dead. But, what was not known and what could never be known, was that he was responsible for his death.

The screams Wilf heard during the night had not been a dream but the most dreadful of realities and a small part of the nightmare that would haunt him for the rest of his life.

CHAPTER THIRTEEN –
THE SEARCH CONTINUES

SATURDAY 5 JULY 1941

After Bill had delivered his bairns to Elsie and Archie's house at the bottom of the road he walked the streets of the Hill alone and knocked on almost every door of every house in the village. He even knocked on the one half way down the street where a loner lived who did all manner of unusual things and enjoyed frightening the living daylights outta bairns and grownups alike. The bloke regularly smelt of the Devil's brew, and when under the influence of drink became a classic example of 'ale in an' brains out'. Bill also thought however a drunken man often spoke a sober mind. Only the week before the soft sod had stuck his head outta his front door with his face plastered in white flour and what looked like ruby red lipstick on every inch of skin below his nose. It shocked a couple of boys half to bloody death and their Father threatened to hit the bloke aback the neck with a stocking full of shit if he ever did anything like it again. So the man had gone underground and been as still and as quiet as the grave for almost a week. No bugger had seen hide or hair of him. Some said that there was no harm in the bloke apart from the fact that his head was full of shit an' after all there were all sorts in a box of liquorice. Undeterred, Bill knocked firmly on his door and braced himself not knowing what to expect if he answered and hoping he wouldn't be as drunk as a skunk if he did. Nobody came to the door so Bill carried on working his way down the street and knocking firmly on every door in his path. To their credit, people who were at home opened their doors as wide as they could in their eagerness to help. Their hearts reached out to him as he searched the village for his lad. Sparks of hope occasionally flickered as people welcomed him into their homes to hear first-hand accounts from Kenneth's playmates of where they had been and what they had been up to all day. Anxious parents looked on in shock and disbelief. In one house a young boy, Harold, was firmly held by his ear lobe whilst his Father threatened him:

"Now tell Mr Hackney the truth about anything you have seen or heard to do with young Kenneth. If you don't, I'm warning you, I'll give you what for and you won't be able to sit down or scratch your arse for a bloody week!" The interrogation continued.

It was obvious that the lad, flinching in pain whilst his ear turned bright red, knew little or nothing at all about Kenneth's whereabouts. But the villagers combined, almost as one in their eagerness to help. They had everything in common and shared most things, including their poverty and their pain. None of them was exempt from the intensity of fear and foreboding surrounding the possibility of losing one of their boys. Fear had well and truly spread her net and her presence engulfed the entire village as rumours spread like wildfire igniting questions and assumptions that had no easy answers or solutions. 'Had someone taken him and if so, who, why and what for?' Every community had its share of shady characters. Laggards and lazy sods that nobody would dare turn their backs on and Golden Hill was no exception. It had a few of 'em, sure enough, and even Bill found himself thinking twice before knocking on a couple of the dubious doors. Such reservations did not stop him in his pursuit as he cast caution to the wind. He was on a mission and would find his lad if it became the last thing he ever did.

A couple of boys told Bill they had seen Kenneth, even played with him for a while in Wilson's Wood but didn't know where he had gone when they had separated and left in opposite directions. Bill felt as if he was collecting ill-fitting pieces from different jigsaws and had no chance of ever joining them together to make a clear picture. All the bits and pieces combined didn't amount to anything very much or make an ounce of common sense. No one could throw any light on where his boy was and what had happened to him. It seemed as if he had vanished into thin air; disappeared. Missing and lost were the most dreaded of words since the outbreak of war. They were words that instinctively released Fear's most treacherous tentacles as she adopted a vice-like grip, as powerful as that of a boa constrictor crushing the life out of its prey before swallowing it whole. But on this day Lost did not mean 'Lost at Sea' and neither did 'Missing' have anything to do with 'Missing in Action'. Today, the frightening words were being banded about in relation to a boy; Kenneth, a nine-year old blonde curly haired lad who seemed to be both missing and lost.

Behind every closed door families were instinctively drawn closer together. Some demonstrated more warmth to each other that night than they had managed to for a very long time. Every home struggled in an attempt to make ends meet. Supplying enough food for their tables and their broods' bellies was a constant concern as many juggled scraps of food and spread their butter thin in order to make a little seem like a lot and go a long way. Finding sufficient clothes for the backs of their children became an art form in itself. Old curtains were cut up and made into skirts and dresses for the girls and flannel was used to make short trousers for the boys. Families with treadle sewing machines did roaring trades. Somewhere along the line basic necessities became number one priorities leaving kisses and cuddles often in short supply. It was not that the children were not loved but survival became paramount and persistently possessed the minds of those who had been left at home to fight the war on the home front draining both their time and their energies. It was a constant battle and all they could do to keep their heads above the ever-swelling waters of need and deprivation. Many families could be heard singing together under the dim glow of gaslight mantles in subconscious attempts to liven their spirits. Renditions of 'Over the Rainbow' 'When you Wish upon a Star' and 'It's a Hap-Hap-Happy Day' bounced around the terraced hovels of the village and to some ears sounded like the worst form of satirical propaganda imaginable that belied the reality of their awful circumstances. On this night however the majority of families on the Hill were secretly relieved that it was not their bairn, not their little boy that was missing. Children were irreplaceable and there wasn't one family on the Hill that didn't have their awareness of this truth raised a peg or two as they saw Bill walking the streets in search of his missing lad.

Nobody in the village could quite equate to what was happening and unfolding before their very eyes. Friends could only begin to imagine the feelings that engulfed Kenneth's parents and his family. A child reported missing in the village was unheard of. There had to be some ordinary explanation, a simple solution and neighbours, behind closed doors, discussed a range of possibilities and explanations. 'Perhaps he was hiding somewhere. Perhaps he'd fallen out with one of his mates and gone off in a strop on his own, doing his own thing in misplaced defiance. Perhaps he was hiding in an air-raid shelter. Had anyone thought of looking in them all? What about searching the outside toilets and coalhouses at the bottom of the narrow cobbled backyards?' the village pondered but came to no conclusions.

Summer became more like winter overnight in the village. Everyone was prepared for war, for air raids, for rationing but this was a different kind of enemy altogether. At such times Catholics, Primitive Methodists, Wesleyan Methodists and Protestants all united as one in prayer and, on this occasion, to pray for the safe return of the lad. Church attendance had increased a hundred-fold since the outbreak of war and 'men of the cloth' had, at last, in some opinions, found themselves with full-time jobs. Friends and neighbours lit candles in the Catholic Church, others simply wrote 'Kenneth' on a prayer card and popped it into a box, others called on St Christopher to keep the lad safe and help him find his way home whilst others set about doing what they practically could by checking outside toilets and coalhouses. Some, on the other hand, thought it to be a storm in a teacup that would soon blow over and prove to be a lot of fuss about nothing. And yet there must be someone, somewhere, who knew the truth of it all. Who knew what had happened to the blonde curly haired lad and where he was.

The small search party of weary and hard-working men all returned to Bill and Nell's empty-handed. No trace of Kenneth anywhere apart from the Black's lad who had told Sam Squires that he'd seen him in Wilson's Wood. The search party had all hoped all assumed that the lad would be safe back at home when they returned from their search. They each expected someone else to have found him and, if need be, to have carried him kicking and screaming home. But there was no such find, no such luck and every man turned to home with the heaviest of hearts and painting the most forlorn of pictures. Every one of the party was regarded as a rough man, even fodder for the battlefield, but they were Bill's mates, his drinking partners and although many of them were uneducated and as rough as bears' arses they had hidden deep inside their rough exteriors the hearts of lions and the word failure did not exist in a lion's vocabulary. In fact World War 1 had recorded them as 'lions that had been led by donkeys'. Lions whose incompetent leaders had not been fit to tie their fearless boot laces. United, they could not rest. Could not relax, could not give up on the search until the lad was safe under his own roof. They would not be beaten so decided to regroup, adopt a different tack and search again.

"Let's focus on Wilson's Wood where Sam Squires said he'd been playin' with one of the Black's lads" someone in the group shouted up. This remark spearheaded an almost unanimous decision, quickly reinforced on the back of the premise that wherever Kenneth was they had somehow missed him and would surely find him the second-time round. The determined force moved off to search again.

Bill left the front door to their house open just a little as he walked through into the middle room. He told the neighbours that he would leave it open and not to bother knocking if they thought of anything to tell him, anything at all, no matter how insignificant it might seem. And so Bill sat in the middle room, stunned, motionless, waiting for someone, anyone, to turn up with news of his son. After all, some bugger somewhere must have seen something.

Nell busied herself cutting strips of old cloth to use in her next pegged rug. The existing one was full of holes caused by red hot cinders which had fallen off the fire and burnt straight through the rug before being retrieved and returned to the flames by a set of well-used fireside tongues. The rug literally stank of dust, dirt and debris. No amount of beating and thrashing it on the line in the backyard had been able to remove it or freshen it up. The dirt and dust was ground in. So, even though pegging was hard on the fingers, hands and wrists Nell decided to make a new rug in an attempt to brighten up the hearth and her spirit. She cut equally sized strips of cloth about two inches wide by two feet long then folded them over between her fully extended finger and thumb before cutting them through the folds to make shorter strips for pegging. She kept them as small as she could so that the strips went farther and covered as big an area of the sack as possible. She had got the old sack ready to peg a few days earlier. She designed it and marked it out by drawing diamonds in its four corners and etching a circle in its perceived centre. She relished the use of old woollen coats for this purpose and the eligible bachelor, Mr Cooke, whose collars she washed, starched and ironed, had given her a dark blue pure wool overcoat. He may as well have given her the name of the winner in the Grand National for the thrill it gave her. A pure wool coat! Taking possession of it was incentive enough to start to peg a completely new rug from scratch. There would be no need to repair the old one. It was going to be out with the old and in with the new. Only a few days before, she had been feeling so very excited at the prospect of working on it and yet, today, there was not a shred of excitement in her entire body. Her heart was as heavy as the old pegged rug itself, the one that it took two of 'em to lift off the middle room floor. She tried to stay focused on the job in hand. She knew that one coat wouldn't be enough to cover the whole sack so she would need to use what rags she had saved as well. She would keep the strips of blue wool coat for the centre circle, the same colour cloth for the four diamonds and anything leftover would be pegged into the in-between sections just as long as the sack was completely covered without a fraction of an inch of it showing through. Her peg was oiled and ready to start work. She deftly used it to pull the individual strips of the old coat in and through the sack one at a time. Every squeak of the small spring in the peg echoed around the empty room but she needed to keep herself busy, fully occupied. With every strip of the old overcoat she pulled through the sack she hoped that it would be her last and that she would not need to peg for distraction very much longer because her lad, her boy, would be home soon and everything would return to normal.

CHAPTER FOURTEEN –

DAYDREAMS AND NIGHTMARES

It was late into the evening when Bill returned home empty handed and his children, minus Kenneth, were tucked up in some bugger else's bed. He appreciated the offer of help from unexpected quarters and although the acceptance of it felt alien to him he was, nonetheless, grateful to the hand that had been extended to them in their hour of need. His heart was well and truly in the bottom of his worn-out boots. To the unknowing eye Bill's boots appeared to be anything but worn out. In fact, a person could almost see their own reflection in the shine he achieved by copious amounts of spit, polish and brushing and belied their true condition. Bill's boots, although blacked and polished on the top had thick pieces of cardboard hidden deep inside them to protect his feet from the gaping holes in the soles of both feet. Everyone knew that you could read a man by the appearance of his shoes so Bill made sure no bugger would ever know, by looking at the top of his, that they had great big bloody holes in both their soles. No, he made damn sure no bugger would ever guess that. He said that they could look as close as they wanted to at 'em cuz all they'd see was the reflection of their own bloody face shining back.

"Could I have another word Mr Hackney please?" It was PC Shaw the young police officer who was still on a wild goose chase and a hiding for nothing. "I've been investigating the discrepancies I spoke to you about earlier surrounding your son's whereabouts" he continued without looking Bill straight in the eye. The bobby had appeared yet again outta thin air and was standing in the house as bold as brass. He was like a bad bloody penny that kept turnin' up uninvited. 'What on earth was he doing stood in his middle room again, the cheeky young whipper-snapper' Bill thought to himself but quickly remembered, in half a trance, that he had left the front door open a little. He therefore gave the young PC the benefit of the doubt as he concluded that he must have knocked on the door before entering the house but because he had been miles away, deep in thought he had not heard him. As well as leaving the door open to encourage neighbours to pop in Bill also thought it might have made it easier for Kenneth, especially if he had just been playing a game on everyone, to sneak back in without having to get past the barrier that knocking would have created. But the open door had only invited the young irritating police officer to pass underneath its lintel and beyond its doorposts. Bill did not want to welcome him into his home and really regretted providing the police force with a bloody open invitation.

PC Shaw's presence filled the middle room just as uncomfortably as his immature head tried to fill his hard blue helmet. He told Bill he had been studying the pages of his routine but makeshift notes made earlier that day and thought that things did not quite add up. In truth, he was finding it difficult to a make head or a tail out of his informal interview notes. His records seemed to disagree, contradict findings and worse still there was no definite thread to follow or trace. One minute Kenneth was recorded as being seen at one end of the village and then reported as being seen by someone else, at the same time, at the other end of the Hill. 'So unless there were two of 'em, twin boys, then the lad could not have been in two places at the same bloody time. Could he now?' he concluded as if resting what he thought was his case.

"I'm totally confused by it all" he said whilst scratching his forehead underneath his helmet with the tip of his pencil. He seemed to be very uncomfortable indeed in his oversized helmet and uniform. Bill remembered thinking that the poor lad was sweating like a bloody pig and that fact alone would have contributed to any bugger's confusion. On the other hand he also thought that 'it wouldn't have taken very much to confuse such a wet-behind-ears Officer, now would it? Confused by it all, my arse! What the bloody hell did he think him and Nell were feelin' like? What an utter and complete waste of time!' Bill managed to outwardly portray respect for the lad's office and humoured him as best he could in the most frustrating and frightening of circumstances.

Finally the young officer managed to get to the point and told Bill he had just needed to check that the lad was not at home before going over some ground again and revisiting a couple of witnesses. The officer was finding it difficult to put any meat on the disjointed bones of his informal investigations and silently hoped to God that the enquiries did not turn formal or else he'd find himself half way down the Swannee River without a bloody paddle! 'If he couldn't understand his notes, then nobody else would, would they?' He fought to retain an air of composure even though he was nearing the end of his shift.

How Bill wished his lad had turned up. How he wished he could have turned round to the PC and smugly said: 'Thanks very much Officer but it's all sorted. It's all been exaggerated, blown outta all proportion. As you can see the lad's home fit and well. Safe and sound! He'd just been playin' a joke on us all, a Hide-n-Seek game that he roguishly overplayed. 'He's sorry for all the fuss, aren't you, son?' he pondered as he imagined himself looking at his boy who'd still have a twinkle of mischief in one of his bright blue eyes.

Instead Bill couldn't think of anything at all to say to the Constable. He just nodded in acknowledgement and recognition of what had been relayed to him and almost immediately and subconsciously nodded again as if in personal resignation and submission to the truth, to the absolute awful truth and reality of it all.

The young PC tucked his notebook back into his top pocket together with his head-scratching pencil and firmly buttoned them both down as he resigned himself to the fact that he would be working late on what he still believed would end up being an absolute waste of time and good money.

After Bill saw the invading police officer out of his home he refused to close the front door behind him and left it open slightly wider. 'Surely Kenneth would be watching from a safe distance somewhere. Perhaps he had seen them all looking for him from the security of his hiding place. If so, then he must have seen his Father walking the streets, knocking on doors, and calling out his name. Perhaps his boy had wanted to run back home but been too afraid to. Perhaps he'd seen and heard the army of men searching for him and feared the repercussions if he just turned up after pulling off a prank, a simple joke that had turned unexpectedly sour. 'Or maybe', Bill continued to contemplate, 'and more than likely, he might well have been too afraid to have simply turned up for fear of the punishment he would have received from the back of Nell's hand. Bill wondered if his lad naively believed her when she had recently threatened to hit him so hard that he'd wake up in the middle of next week. And who, in their right mind, would want to come home to face such a good hiding?' Of course, Nell would never have done such a thing, but to hear her bellow and threaten it was enough in itself to do the trick and more than enough to send shivers down the back of a six foot six man let alone that of a nine-year old boy.

With the children, including baby Terrence, farmed out at the Williams's house Nell struggled to settle. She was unable to bear the weight of the pegged rug across her knees any longer and grew increasingly anxious. She had not been able to settle to anything. She picked up her crochet and hook several times only to put them back down again, only to pick them back up again as she repositioned her rocking chair in order to face the mantelpiece clock and wait. She could crochet without any concentration whatsoever. She did not need to think about what she was doing because, somewhere along the line, it had become second nature to her. She too found herself thinking about the heavy-handed way she often disciplined her brood. 'Was she really too hard on them?' she wondered. She thought that everyone knew, only too well, that to 'spare the rod', resulted in 'spoiling the child' and she would never be accused of that. She would rather knock some sense into their thick heads whilst, at the very same time, loving them with a real and almost consuming passion. Nell had paid her dues into a community and country culture. A way of life forged during the harshness and necessities of war. A society wherein it was assumed, rightly or wrongly, that it would do no good at all to handle bairns with kid gloves or wrap 'em up in cotton wool and tissue paper. In fact, it was widely believed that it wouldn't do 'em any favours whatsoever nor an ounce of good to give 'em a soft upbringing, none whatsoever. Surprisingly, Nell proved to be an angel when compared with her counterparts and her approach to discipline. That very day one of her neighbours had shouted half way down the street to one of her bairns "If you don't come back now I'll knock seven shades a shit out a yer when yer bloody do" and there was not an ounce of doubt in her threat. Nell didn't have a swinging brick in place of a heart and considered herself on a par with Mother Nature herself who was only ever cruel to be kind. She had her own boundaries and beliefs and lived within them regardless of her neighbours' stance and customs. And so she rocked herself backwards and forwards, as she glued her eyes on the clock, crocheted and waited. She prepared Kenneth a supper of tripe and onions, and even though it wouldn't be a special Sunday the next day she had already decided to open a tin of Spam as a treat and to help pour oil on troubled waters. 'Yes, that's what she planned to do on the 'morrow. She'd make Spam butties. As for today, well her lad's supper was ready and waitin' for him and he'd be in for it soon'. In fact she would have given him the very food off her own plate and the plates of every bugger else for that matter if he came home. As soon as he showed-up and after she had held him close to her heart and fed him, washed him and put him to bed she would give him what for and probably not quite in that order. She hoped and prayed that when he did come home it would not be too late to fetch her other bairns back from Elsie's. She didn't like the thought of 'em sleeping under another's roof. They belonged with her, all of 'em, together, a family. It didn't feel right; everything was disjointed and out of sync.

The police station, visited earlier in the day by Annie Jones, who had, only out of the goodness of her heart, reported Kenneth missing, was positioned towards the top of the High Street, directly opposite a small farmyard. It was an imposing red brick, double-fronted building with equally imposing double doors at its centre. Once inside it had a cold-feel waiting area, rather like the atmosphere of waiting rooms in train stations, or, Bill imagined, as cold as one of the new-fangled electric refrigerators that were becoming commonplace in America. A small counter desk was situated slap bang in the middle of the waiting room. The desk clearly separated two very distinct areas of the station. It was thought that a person was safe if they stayed on the right side of the law by staying on the right side of the mesh-encased counter.

Bill had never crossed over the threshold that separated the two halves of the station and was determined that none of his kith and kin would step over it either. In fact, he habitually did all he could to keep his family on the straight and narrow. Everyone knew, only too well, that the road to destruction was broad and normally there were no U turns anywhere down its one-way path. All his little brood were taught the importance of being polite and rigorously practised their manners in all situations. They could spout please, thank you, excuse me and pardon me off by heart. Manners had been drilled into them by the rote learning method. 'After all, everyone knew that 'manners can make a man and good manners cost nothin', didn't they?' It also meant that Bill could take his children anywhere and feel proud of them. They knew how to behave in company and 'woe-betide any of 'em if they didn't do so' he regularly half boasted and half warned. He did however firmly hold to the tenet that in adult company, children should be seen and not heard and should always 'let their meat shut their mouths'

176

at the dinner table and ask 'please may I leave the table' when they had finished their meal even if it had only been fried-up leftovers of bubble and squeak from the previous day.

Nell also kept her bairns busy by assigning them a regular variety of jobs to complete with diligence and take more than a measure of pride in. Underneath the surface, however, there was always more than one method in her madness. She believed in the saying that the devil makes work for idle hands and so she made damn sure that she kept all her bairns busy and thereby out of mischief and falling foul to the wrong side of the law. Bill, with every ounce of strength he could find, ensured that his family would make their way in the world by hard work and honest means. In doing so, he trusted that they would always be able to hold their heads up among the best of the bunch. He tried, in spite of the evidence to the contrary, to teach his children that all men were born equal and that they should neither feel compelled to look up at or down on another person. Positions of office commanded respect from all quarters and not necessarily, the people who held the office. In spite of this philosophy, Bill knew only too well that it would only be a matter of time before his brood crossed paths with 'eye-brows' who might try to laud it over them, intimidate or suppress them, albeit unintentionally in an attempt to make them feel like second-class citizens. He thought that if such people were allowed to win their battle of the classes, then there was a danger that they might crush his brood's individual characters and personalities by using a force as heavy as any hammer striking an impenetrable anvil. Bill watched the forging of metal every day. The smelter, the shaping of it until, eventually, it was hammered into something else. So just in case some fancy-arsed bugger wanted to reshape his kids, rob them of their individuality, dignity and pride he had a back-up plan. Faced with prejudice of this nature he told all his bairns, in no uncertain terms, that if ever they felt intimidated, crushed and about to crumble and fall, to remember his words:

"Thait worth ten of them buggers. Now act like it. Deep breath, head up and shoulders back and bloody shine. Dazzle 'em with your brightness. You're unique and as good, if not better, than all them fancy-arsed lot put together. Don't let 'em cripple and disable you. Be what you were meant to be and more. You may be working-class but that does not make you second best. You might be a small cog in a big machine but you still have a reason and a purpose in life so go out and bloody find it cuz at the end of the game every bugger knows that the King and the Pawn go back in the same bloody box."

So with one eye on Nell and the other on the clock Bill put his head back and started to map out his family's future. His children were so very different from each other; no two peas in a pod. They were all special in their own very different ways and all equally treasured and valued. He rested his head on the high-backed chair as he visualised his children.

Terrence his youngest bairn was the baby of his brood. With the best will in the world he couldn't possibly know what might lie ahead in life for him. He did however find it comforting to think that his babe might one day travel the world. Learn first-hand by seeing and experience; be handed the opportunity to absorb the beauty of the world in peaceful times. Bill had been a First World War soldier and only seen the destruction and devastation of the places he was commissioned to serve his country in. He fought for the freedom of his bairns and the bairns of others in the hope that they would stand on his shoulders and the shoulders of bigger and better men than himself, men who had given their all for tomorrow's families in the hope that they would enjoy life and liberty and soak up the beauty of the world as it was meant to be. Countries and countryside unspoilt by the degradation and deprivations of war. War, which had brought in its train epidemics of death, disease and destruction. So perhaps Terrence, his youngest, would have the best chance outta all his bairns to circle the globe and travel to the other side of the world. Perhaps he would not be forced to enlist, to serve his country or be faced with the stigma and repercussions of declaring himself a conscientious objector. Maybe he would see the world and life beyond the boundaries of the tightly packed terraces of Golden Hill. Perhaps he would. He hoped he would and 'there was nothing wrong with hopin' now was there?'

Billy, the next and the son named after him. He wanted so much outta life for him, more than he had known himself. One thing was for sure, he definitely didn't want young Bill to be forced to wear shoes with cardboard stuck inside 'em in order to cover up the holes in their soles. No way did he want that for him or any of his bairns. He would like Bill to own the best pair of shoes any bugger's money could possibly buy. Even crocodile ones! He'd recently read something about crocodile shoes. Never actually seen a pair, but read about 'em. He'd said it before and he'd say it again, 'you could tell a lot about a man by looking at his shoes' and what about overcoats for that matter? He'd looked on, silently envious, as he saw Nell cut Mr Cooke's navy blue pure wool coat into strips to peg into a rug for the hearth. Bill accepted that it was too late for him to ever own a decent overcoat but not too late for his namesake to own one, or two, or three or a bloody wardrobe full. Perhaps he'd even own one made from the finest cashmere with the most luxurious of linings. Now that would be sight for sore eyes. A pure cashmere camel coat with a pair of matching leather brogues! Eyes would pop outta their bloody heads on stalks. Every bugger knew that a man only gets what he pays for in life and Bill wanted the finest and the best that money could buy for his brood and especially for his Bill, his namesake.

Alma was his only wench. She would soon be taught to wash, iron, cook and clean as good and, if Nell had her way, better than all the wenches on the Hill put together. Bill had inconspicuously noticed that Nell was already setting about making sure of it. She was determined to teach her daughter everything she knew and more if she could. Alma already looked out for Billy and helped Nell with changing and scrubbing the bairn's nappy rags. She was a pretty wench and worth a second look by any bloke. Coupled with a range of domestic skills, including the art of making lobby, pies and pastries she would soon make a first-class wife and mother. She'd be as good a catch as any man could reel in outta the local community pool. Men tended not to look farther than their bloody noses for their wives and mothers of their bairns. There was no doubting that Alma would definitely fetch ducks off water when she turned a young woman and doubtless suitors would be queuing up two-double to take her out. But it would have to be some bugger as special as she was if Bill was to walk her down the aisle without an ounce of regret. It would have to be a man deserving of her and not a 'big girl's blouse' of a bloke. He would have to be able to prove that he could keep her well fed and clothed. Bill would make it perfectly clear to him at the off that he would not be having her teeth pulled out afore she married him just to save him money in the future. There'd be no chance of that happenin'. He didn't hold with the practice so the bloke would take her with what teeth she had in her head or not at all. In fact, Bill hoped Alma stayed with him 'til she was good and ready for a life of marriage and motherhood. He knew only too well how hard life could be on wenches and agreed with the premise that 'if men had to give birth to bairns then there'd be a bloody lot less of 'em about. In fact the world would probably come to a bloody standstill'.

Wilf, what about his big 'un? He could be a bit of showman at times. Bill was sick at heart that he had not been able to afford him his well-earned and well-deserved grammar school education. He had not doubted the Headmaster when he told him, in no uncertain terms, that his lad was Prime Minister material. 'But, seriously, where was the bloke coming from? In fact, what bloody planet was he on, the bloody moon, and what chance was there of ever going there? Pigs might fly! There was no bloody chance. Elephants flying; now that was another story', Bill's thoughts digressed. He'd heard that Walt Disney was set to release a film later that year about a flying elephant called Dumbo so perhaps nothing was too fairytale and fanciful apart from flying to the moon and back. Yet, with both feet firmly on the ground, there were practical considerations that needed to be taken afore making important decisions. There was always a bigger picture. 'What if he had agreed to let Wilf attend the Grammar School? What if he had scrimped scrapped and sacrificed to pay for the uniform and a multitude of other odds and sods? Enabled him to walk through the School's grand doors and enter another realm, another world. In reality he would have had more chance of walking through the back of a wardrobe to live in Narnia than entering the hallowed halls of the school. Because what would have happened if in just over 2 years' time Kenneth was offered a place there too? He would never have been able to stretch to paying for uniforms and bits and pieces for two of 'em and what he couldn't do for 'em all he wouldn't do for any. They must all be treated fairly and equally.' So, unfair as it might have seemed from every bugger else's narrow perspective, Bill had made the only decision he could ever have made as he viewed the overall spectrum; Prime Minister material or not. Besides, a more realistic road would ultimately prove less disappointing by a mile as he determined to find Wilf a job at the factory where he worked himself. 'Perhaps the war would be over by the time the lad was fourteen and he could start work alongside him in the foundry and be glad of it. He'd speak up for his boy ahead of his birthday and put a good word into the right ear and that would go a long way and carry a lot of weight. Yes, he could easily fix up his big 'un with work and so that just left Kenneth.'

Kenneth was definitely not a leader. He was content to follow others and Bill worried that this might one day lead him into trouble. A boy needed a strong sense of character not to be tempted to run with the pack and have the will and determination to swim against the tide in troubled waters. Kenneth was too easily carried along with flow. Despite his blonde curly hair and blue eyes he was no angel Bill knew that but he wasn't a bad lad either and had a kind, sensitive heart. He could be impish, a bit of a coy rogue with a cheeky smile. Recently, along with a couple of other lads who had led the way he'd been involved in a bit of bother at school ahead of the summer holidays. A couple of 'em had been teasing a few girls in the playground, trying to spoil their skippin' rope fun. One boy went a step too far and pulled one of the wench's pigtails and she went runnin' to the teacher feigning tears and pointed an accusing finger at Kenneth. Without explanation or defence he was given the strap as punishment for one of the other boy's crimes but none of 'em ever owned up to the truth of it including Kenneth.

So, without a whimper, Kenneth took the strap for another culprit, an act so typical of him. Bill was also not ignorant to the fact that Kenneth leaned and relied heavily on his big brother and decided that he would put a stop to it sooner rather than later and definitely before Wilf started work. If it was to be the last thing he did Bill vowed to teach Kenneth how to stand on his own two feet, to follow no bugger's lead and stand in no bugger's shadow; even the big 'un cast by his hero of a brother. He would help him to unearth the courage he needed to enable him to set his own course, to steer and shape his own life. He knew his lad could draw and paint. He'd seen his etchings and had to admit that they were damn good. He agreed that his lad had a talent but there was no brass in it and he'd find him a proper job when the time came. If nothing else came along for his lads then they would all follow him in his foundry footsteps. 'Hard work never hurt any bugger, did it?'

Just as Bill's eyes started to close in around his daydreams for his children he was catapulted back into reality by the raised voice of Sergeant Pierce, PC Shaw's superior officer. "Evening Mr Hackney. Can I have a word please?" His request was shouted through the almost wide-open front door and into the empty parlour. Bill jumped to his feet as if standing to attention, bolted back to reality without a full second having passed on the mantelpiece clock. His feet moved automatically towards the voice of the Sergeant. As soon as Bill laid eyes on him he knew there was an air of formality about him and he reeked of official business. Bill beckoned the serious and solemn faced Sergeant through into the middle room. They both walked past the pantry under the stairs containing the family's tummy-hole stash. Bill remembered thinking that he was relieved that they had nothing to hide. No contraband would ever have been found under his roof if they searched it from top to bottom all day and all bloody night.

"Would you like to sit down Sir? I have news about your boy", the Sergeant quite simply said as if reading from a transcript or a well-rehearsed line from a stage play. The words bounced around the walls of the cluttered middle room as Bill in surrender slumped into the chair positioned next to Nell's rocker. Although they did not speak to each other Nell and Bill both wanted exactly the same thing. They wanted to put a stop on what was happening to them; put the brakes on and put an end to the roller coaster ride in mid air. They wanted to disembark but everything was running wild and was well and truly outside of their control. The Sergeant, still standing bolt upright, continued:

"I'm very sorry to have to tell you this but PC Shaw discovered the body of a young boy just a short while ago." The only word Bill heard, the only word that he wanted to hear and that registered in his muzzy mind was the word 'young' so he hopefully asked "What do you mean by young Sergeant, two or three?" and continued without taking a breath. "If so, then it couldn't be our lad, our Kenneth, could it? He's nine. You know that don't you?" 'Nine wasn't young, was it?' Bill silently reasoned with himself. His boy was nine not two or three. Sadly,

Bill's reckoning did not deter the Sergeant. It did not make him alter his course of action neither did it make him correct himself by withdrawing his well-rehearsed words. It did not redirect him in his mission nor make him apologise for having made a terrible mistake. The firm faced Sergeant with the sturdiest of stiff upper lips was unrelenting in his duty: "Sir, would you be kind enough to accompany me to the police station please? We've got the lad there and we need someone to identify his body before he can be moved".

'What in the name of God Almighty was he talking about? The man must be as mad as a bloody hatter an' as daft as a bloody brush. He could see where young PC Shaw got his stupidity from, by following his Sergeant's bloody example.' Bill's thoughts somersaulted and tumbled around in his head and when he subconsciously added 'em all up they still didn't make a penny worth of sense.

Nell let out the most awful of stifled sounds. Stifled because her hands, that had instinctively dropped the crochet hook, had both been raised to simultaneously cover her mouth. Her worst nightmare had started to unfold and be played out in front of her very eyes as she realised and acknowledged her helplessness to face the ugly ultimatum. 'Could something dreadful, terrible really have happened to her bairn, her blonde curly haired lad?' Nell thought whilst reluctantly relinquishing more than half an inch of ground in her fight to keep faith and hope alive as she submitted to the possibility that Fear may not have darkened her door alone. Not for the first

186

time that day, Nell sensed Death alongside her, almost breathing down her neck, even though, for the time being at least, He remained hidden, within Fear's shadow.

"Dear God, it isn't true. It can't be true" she gasped whilst at the same time she struggled to take in sufficient air to enable her to keep breathing as normally as possible. Her lungs were starved of oxygen as panic controlled her entire body and possessed her mind.

"Is there anyone I can get to come and sit with you, Mrs Hackney?" the Sergeant asked in hushed tones. "A neighbour, a friend perhaps. What about family? Can we call on some of your family? Send a telegraph perhaps."

'Thait 'ave a hard job' Nell thought. She had little or no family living within arm's reach. Her family had settled in different parts of the country years before when her ancestors landed together in England from Athy in Southern Ireland in an attempt to escape the 1849 potato famine. So there was no close family to be summoned or called upon. Besides, Nell was used to being fetched herself to help in more emergencies than she cared to remember and bucked at the thought of calling on anyone to help her. She was fiercely independent. 'She didn't need any bugger's help. It was all a mistake anyway. It could not be true; it was not her lad. She would not need anyone. They could all sod-off whoever they were' her mind defiantly raced. She just wanted to lock the doors and hide behind the security of the blackout curtains. Hide from the faces of every bugger in the street. 'No there was no bugger she wanted the Sergeant to call or to fetch or to tell his bloody blatant lies to.'

"Do you need a coat?" Mr Hackney. 'Coat, a coat' thought Bill. 'What the hell was he on about? What would he need a coat for?' But Nell in automatic mode stood, opened the pantry door and reached in for Bill's working coat. She wrapped it around his shoulders and with tears silently making their way down her tired face she buttoned it up across his broad chest. In more than half a daze she didn't notice that she had fastened the buttons into the wrong buttonholes creating a lopsided ill-fitting coat across Bill's drooping shoulders. Shoulders that over many years had felt the strain, but never once gave way; almost akin to Atlas, whose shoulders took the weight of the world across the nape of his neck. It could have been argued that the weight of the world, even the world at war, would have been a lighter option for Bill to carry. His entire body was heavy, weighted down; heavier than it had ever felt before, even during, the First World War. Yes, the weight of the world couldn't possibly have felt as heavy as the burden Bill was being asked to bear.

Just as the last sliver of the evening sun set over the village, just as her last rays of red and gold shed their light across the hill of gorse and buttercups, Bill and Sergeant Pierce left the house. Deliberately, and as quietly as he could, Sergeant Pierce closed the door behind them. There would be no point leaving it open. 'The lad would not be coming home tonight' he thought. 'In fact, he would not be coming home ever again.'

They walked up the uneven back streets towards the police station together, side by side. Bill who had walked the streets only a few hours earlier searching for his boy knew them all like the back of his hand. The cardboard in his boots had almost worn away and as they walked past the cobbler's shop Bill wondered what it would feel like to have new soles expertly fitted onto the bottoms of his one and only pair of boots. But he knew only too well that he would never know what that luxury felt like and that he'd be cutting and shaping pieces of cardboard just as soon as he could and be grateful for it. Money was needed for food and his boots were too good to be used alongside the slack stacked on the middle room fire just yet.

CHAPTER FIFTEEN - AN INQUEST

Bill did not know how his legs carried him the never-ending distance between his house and the police station. He thought they would give way underneath him as they trembled ever so slightly and almost reminiscent of how they had first trembled with fear in the Belgium trenches during the war. He had more than played his part in the first war. The war that had been boldly declared was the war to end to all wars. 'What an absolute joke!' he thought. 'As long as men had holes in their arses there would be wars' he deliberated as he felt the first chill of the night send a shiver down his back. He pulled his ski-wiff coat tighter across his body and gripped it for all it was worth. He hoped Sergeant Pierce hadn't noticed his hands tremble and in doing so assumed him a coward. Although in very different circumstances than those on the front-line of the battlefield, he did not want him to think he had a yellow streak down the middle of his back, not tonight, not on any night. He decided that he would brave head on whatever he found waiting for him at the station and stand his ground just as he had in the war. He wouldn't do a runner. He wouldn't desert. He would never be classed as one of the poor sods who were led out and shot blind-folded for cowardice at dawn. Not him, he was prepared to stand steady, eyeball his enemy whatever shape or form it took. 'So whatever he found waiting for him at the station, he would face it with every bone in his body braced for the worst. He would do his duty. He would not waiver even though he already knew full well that it wasn't his lad.' Bill could not control his thinking. His thinking was controlling him and raced way ahead of him.

Inside the station Sergeant Pierce lifted the section of the counter that separated the two distinct sides and for the first time in his life Bill stepped over the invisible line to enter the wrong side of the law. As he did so he momentarily looked at two posters that were pinned on the walls either side of the door. The posters served as a reminder to everyone who entered the station that the country was at war. On the left hand side he half glanced at Fougasse's Ministry of Information poster with its background wallpaper displaying cartoon faces of Adolf Hitler whilst, in the foreground, two women sat gossiping together over a table. The words:

'DON'T FORGET THAT WALLS HAVE EARS!

CARELESS TALK COSTS LIVES'

was the poster's stern warning. Bill heard that Fougasse, who was the art editor of the magazine Punch when war broke out, had almost immediately offered his services free to the British government and, as a result, produced propaganda material for almost every ministry. The poster displayed on the opposite wall had quite different connotations and pictured five airmen with the simple words from one of Churchill's most famous speeches:

'NEVER WAS SO MUCH OWED BY SO

MANY TO SO FEW'

and referred, of course, to the airmen who had fearlessly fought to win victory in the skies during the brave battle of Britain the year before. Its message was even more poignant to the local community because Reginald Mitchell, the designer of the Spitfire plane, the very plane that proved to be the salvager of the skies was born in a small village nearby. Although Mitchell had sadly only lived long enough to see a prototype fly his genius, evenly balanced with his humility, did the locals and the country proud. In fact, in Bill's mind, there was no doubt that the community and the country owed a local lad a huge debt of gratitude and one that it would never be able to pay back in a million and one bloody years.

"This way" the Sergeant said as he gently led Bill by the arm through to the back of the station. They walked down what seemed an unending corridor of walls clothed in black and white tiles that formed a perfectly symmetrical pattern only broken by a succession of firmly closed doors on both sides. As they neared the end of the corridor to his horror Bill's thoughts ran ahead of him again:

'The lad's in a cell! They've put him in a cell' he thought in disbelief. 'Cells were for criminals, weren't they? What the hell had a child done to warrant this?' As the door opened the Sergeant put his hand in the centre of

192

Bill's back as if ushering him into a picture palace or music hall seat. They entered a small, bare cold room. North facing Bill remembered thinking. Right in the middle of the cell, almost dead centre, was, what seemed to be an everyday type of table and on it lay a small body, the motionless body of a young child. 'It was probably a boy', Bill thought, 'he'd give the Sergeant the benefit of that, but it was definitely not his lad'. He could tell that a mile off. Everything but the child's face and head was covered, concealed by a mucky-looking off-white sheet but Bill could still tell, he was certain, that it was not Kenneth. 'This boy was a diminutive figure, in comparison to his lad, no more than five or six at the most' Bill concluded, his mind churning through information at a super fast speed.

Mercifully, and probably the only thing in the cell's favour, was the fact that it had high blacked-out windows and although covered by iron bars it meant that nobody could see in or out of the cell. The Sergeant and Bill were closed in, shielded from the eyes of the world. Protected from pity and pain but not unfortunately from the most shocking of truths.

Bill felt relief flood his body and in so doing restore strength to his weakened legs. His lungs filled with air. He stood up straight. The weight he was carrying that had felt as heavy as the world itself rolled immediately off the back of his neck. One glance was enough. He knew straight away that it wasn't Kenneth. 'Thank God. It wasn't him. The child looked nothing like his boy' he muttered.

'This lad, this poor lad lying on a fit for nothing table in the middle of a dismal police cell had dark hair didn't he?' he silently interrogated himself. 'Why had that bloody stupid Police Sergeant fetched him up here? To this God forsaken hole. Everyone and his dog knew only too well that his lad had a mop of blonde curly hair. The daft buggers' he thought as, with a hint of a lilt in his voice, he said: "No, it's not my lad. Seems like you've had me on a hidin' for nothing Sergeant Pierce! Yes, a hiding for bloody nothing that's exactly what your young PC said it would be all along. It's definitely not my lad".

"Please step forward Bill and take a closer look at the lad" was the only response he received in answer to his overtly exuberant statement. And so Bill stepped forward closer to the boy's body as if obeying the officer's command to the letter. He had been a man under authority and knew, without question or reserve, how to do exactly as he was told.

Bill found himself looking at a face that initially reminded him of one of Madame Tussaud's macabre creations housed in the Chamber of Horrors in Marylebone Road, London. The child's face, illuminated by the Ediswan electric light bulb, was swollen and in places bruised black and blue as if it had been beaten and battered with a truncheon. Steadying himself, in an attempt to absorb more detail, Bill noticed swirls of dried dirt on the child's face. He looked closer. It seemed as if the lad's face had been given the once-over with a soap sodden sponge that had worsened its appearance as thick streaks of dirt were caked across his young skin. Bill's eyes moved down over the boy's neck as he followed the dirty lines of rims and ridges left to dry after surplus water had trickled down the boy's swollen cheeks and chin.

Bill stood for what seemed an eternity staring blankly down at the face of the boy. All that went through his mind was that this lad, this poor lad, someone's son, someone's bairn, had dark hair. 'It was not his Kenneth. Thank God Almighty that it was not his lad' he thought. Slowly but instinctively Bill's hand, the hand of a true Father, reached out to touch the boy's head as if to comfort or bless him. For the first time in that eternity of a second Bill audibly gasped as he spotted the finest streak of blonde hair shining its way through a mass of dry brown mud. In that very instant he knew the truth. It was Kenneth, his blonde curly haired son. Sensing his recognition, the Sergeant stepped forward and reached out to touch Bill's shoulder but he shrugged him off. Bill didn't crumble. He put his shoulders back and stood up straight. He refused to pull back the dirty looking sheet that covered his son. He did not need to see any more of his lad's bruised and swollen body but oh how he needed to touch him. Needed to know it was definitely his once full of life full of fun son and not some wax-works creation without a soul or a spirit. Bill slowly and deliberately reached underneath the yellow stained excuse for a sheet searching, grasping for his boy's hand. He grabbed his son's tiny tightly clenched fist, engulfing it, smothering it with a Father's unique protective strength and gentleness. He did not ever want to have to let it go.

He sensed all the love he had for his boy travel through his body, down his arm and into the hand of a corpse, into the shell that was once his blonde curly haired lad. Holding on tightly to his son's hand Bill slowly and deliberately said the words that his worst enemy should never have to utter:

"It's my boy. It's my son, Kenneth. God help us."

Bill left the station refusing all offers of support, not that the Sergeant's custom-made statement 'We'll be in touch just as soon as we know anything more' followed by 'let us know if there is anything we can do to help' and, without pausing to take a breath 'condolences to the wife and rest of the family' amounted to very much. The words seemed empty, shallow, as if spoken as a routine measure and in exactly the same tone and manner as any other police day-to-day business might have been conducted. In his shocked and stunned state Bill wondered what bloody help there could possibly be for him and his family in such a frightful, unbelievable situation. He was unable to absorb very much of the copious formalities that were hurled at him in the station. Words went straight in one ear and straight out the other without the slightest recognition of any registration on his face whatsoever. All Bill could see before him and all he would see for a very long time was the body of his dead boy. 'How on earth could he not have recognised him? It was only his hair, one streak of blonde curly hair, which gave him away' he pondered to himself. 'He must make sure that Nell did not see him in the state he was in. He would do all he could to spare her that much. What an awful, awful tragedy. Who would have thought they would have been in this situation at the start of the run of the mill day? A day he had wrongly assumed would be just like any other day.' Despite everything tumbling around in his head and heart, Bill managed somehow to retain a degree of composure as he subconsciously, automatically, shifted gear into the stiff upper lip mode. He would not break down in front of the Sergeant. He was a man and men did not cry. If he had nothing else he would hold onto his dignity and pride. He thanked the Sergeant for his assistance and asked him to express his gratitude to PC Shaw who had acted above and beyond the call of duty. He strode outside the suffocating station just as confidently as if he had been making his way to a routine shift at the iron and steel works until he turned the corner of the High Street into the protection and darkness of the back alleys. Then, in the doorway of an entry between two terraces he all but crumbled into a heap. His son, his boy was gone from this world and his going had created a cavern within the depths of his heart that was deeper and blacker than any coalmine and one he knew he would have to learn to live with for the rest of his days.

After fighting to regain his composure, he continued to walk towards his home down the empty, dark back streets of the village alone. It was well and truly blackout now in more ways than one. He no longer cared that the pieces of cardboard covering the holes in the soles of his shoes were virtually worn away because he could not feel anything; he was numb from the top of his head to the tips of his toes. He was oblivious to anything and everything around him including the bloody home guard that passed him on the narrow back street and tipped his cap in recognition and politeness. It was nigh impossible to imagine that his heart could humanly sink any lower than it had done in the station. 'How on earth was he going to tell his Nell? Where would he start?' The unthinkable had become a reality. It was the worst nightmare any parent could be asked to exist through. There would be an inquest. He remembered that much from the procedures he had been duly informed about whilst confined in the six by six icebox of a room. The inquest would follow the knife of a post mortem but he refused to think about that. In fact he would never think about it.

When Bill reached the door to his home it was surprisingly still slightly ajar. 'Nell must have reopened it after the Sergeant had gently closed it; as if refusing to relinquish half an expectation, half a hope that her lad would be returning home. How could he possibly tell her that the only way her bairn would be coming home was wrapped in a wooden overcoat which would only happen after the Coroner had released his body for burial? 'How could this nightmare be happening?' Bill thought as he firmly fastened and locked the door behind him as if locking out the night, locking out the prying eyes and gossip, locking out the truth, the pain, the loss.

Nell looked as if she hadn't moved a muscle since Sergeant Pierce had asked Bill to escort him to the station. She was sitting in her rocking chair waiting, just waiting, hoping, trusting and believing that the body of the boy at the station was not her bairn.

She had in fact not stayed sitting in the chair at all but after she had heard the door close behind Bill and the Sergeant, she quickly moved to reopen it so that her lad could easily walk back through it. In a moment of inspiration she had then decided to pick up their family bible from off the top of the tallboy in the corner of the middle room. Before opening it, she wiped away months of dust off its cover and then tentatively searched for Psalm twenty-three. Nell was not a scholar by any stretch of the imagination neither was she a devoutly religious woman. She had seen far too much pain and poverty to ever be that, yet she still believed in something or someone and often read the Shepherd's Psalm in times of extreme difficulty. And so she turned to the page that was worn above all the others in the first section of the book. She stood up as if preparing to make a declaration or oration and although there was barely enough light to read anything by under the dim gas mantles, she deeply inhaled before exhaling and reading out aloud into the emptiness of the room:

"The Lord is My Shepherd, I shall not want;
He maketh me to lie down in green pastures.
He leadeth me beside still waters.
He restoreth my soul.
Yea, though I walk".

At this point her voice broke, trembled and shook with emotion, but she would not be deterred or diverted. She persevered.

"Yea, though I walk....I walk through the valley of the shadow of death".

She paused again, composed herself. She would never have believed that this verse could possibly relate to the loss of her boy. No she would never succumb to that possibility. She stood up straighter, put her shoulders back and lifted her head high. She firmly repeated the words again with as much gusto and boldness as she could:

"though I walk through the valley of the shadow of death".

Her declaration of confidence filled the empty spaces of the room and inadvertently caused Fear herself to turn away and hide within the shadows alongside Charon who withdrew his skeletal hand until they both became camouflaged by the presence of each other.

Nell breathed deeply before she declared:

"I will fear no evil. Do you hear me?" She asked the shadows.
"I will fear no evil" she echoed.
"For Thou art with me
Thy rod and thy staff they comfort me.... They comfort me"

But Nell was unable to finish reading the Psalm and, at this point, before she broke down completely she gently closed the bible and returned it to the top of the tallboy to gather dust again. She almost collapsed into the comfort of her rocking chair with only the mantelpiece clock and the hiss of the gas mantles for company until she heard Bill enter the front room and close the door behind him. She immediately stood to attention as if greeting him from a day's work and tried her best to look straight into his face. She tried to read him; she knew her man as well as she knew the back of her own hand, but his eyes avoided hers and she instinctively knew something was amiss. Without looking directly at her Bill softly said:

"Thait better sit yer down Nell. It's the worst of news I have to tell ya my love. The very worst of news."

Together they somehow managed to stumble their way through the blackest of nights and, in their own individual ways, each stepped into what was to become the deepest and darkest of valleys. Somewhere between night and day in a brief coherent spot Nell and Bill made a pact, an agreement regarding the events that had led up to Kenneth's death. The contents of their verbal contract, forged in the most desperate of circumstances, was only ever heard by the four walls of the house that surrounded them and which had already absorbed the best and the worst of their secrets.

By the time the sun rose and shone across the golden top of the Hill they had agreed on an alliance, a deal, that they hoped would protect the rest of their children, including Wilf, their almost twelve going on twenty-one big 'un. They closed ranks and both firmly decided to do everything within their power to spare their bairns as much upset as they possibly could and to redeem them from as many of the reverberations of the incident as humanly possible. They hoped, as a result of their concurrent accounts, that the only children who would be called to give evidence at the inquest would be the children who had seen their boy die. They would do all within their power to save their bairns the trauma of testifying at their own brother's inquest. The first thing they needed to do, without delay, was to tell their bairns of Kenneth's loss with as little detail as possible before they heard it from other quarters. A tragedy of this nature spread faster than both head lice and impetigo put together. None of them however dared to leave the house until they heard from Sergeant Pierce and so Bill reluctantly reached into the tallboy and extracted a Basildon Bond writing pad and white envelope. The writing paper had no lines printed on it so Bill placed another sheet of paper on which he had drawn a straight black line underneath the sheet he was going to write on to help his writing to stay as straight as possible. He sat down to pen the worst words of his life. Words that no parent should ever have to utter or write down:

Dear Arch 'n Elsie

Sad news I'm afraid. Our Kenneth was found dead late last night and we dunna want our other bairns hearing it from off the street. Please do us the great kindness of tellin' 'em that their brother's gone to be with God in heaven. I trust thee and I'd much rather they heard it from you and your Elsie. We will fetch 'em back just as soon as the police 'ave finished with us. Thank ya.

Bill and Nell.

On the outside of the envelope he simply wrote: To Archie 'n Elsie. He sealed the envelope and waited for a passer-by whom he thought could be trusted to take the letter straight down to the bottom of the street and deliver it into the hand of the addressee and no bugger else. Fortunately, he didn't have to wait long. The street was awake and already had 'itchy ears' curious to know the outcome of the night's events.

The days between the discovery of Kenneth's body and the funeral were an unending blur to Nell and Bill although the pact formed in the darkness of night remained a crystal clear pattern and one that seemed to be going perfectly to plan. Within five days their bubbly boy would have lost his life, been subject to a post mortem and an inquest and be put to rest in a grave, with or without the luxury of a shroud they could not afford to buy.

Bill and Nell were successful in sparing their children from the experiences of being both interviewed by police and summoned to give evidence at their brother's inquest. Together they firmly tapped the cork into the neck of the bottle of truth containing the secrets that led up to Kenneth's disappearance and death and prayed to God that would be the end of it. They wrongly assumed that they would be able to contain the truth and conceal it forever. Ultimately time would prove them wrong simply because Truth finds a way of escaping from all kinds of containers including coffins. She has a distinctive, unique voice and when coupled with Courage she will somehow, somewhere be heard and no amount of corks in no amount of bottles will keep her silent forever.

Bill and Nell however set themselves to stand solidly by their decision, side-by-side, impenetrable, as if forming a shield, a barrier around their depleted brood. Apart from his parents, Wilf never told another living soul his part in the fateful day's events and promised them both, on oath, that he would never disclose the fact that he had been the last person in his family to have seen his brother alive. It was like trying to hide live insects under stones; insects that did not want to be prisoners of the dark forever and would eventually somehow find their own way into the light. The truth was buried six foot under, in a grave in the grounds of the village cemetery alongside the tears of an almost twelve-year old boy who had been too afraid to cry at the death and funeral of his brother and closest friend.

In fact, Nell and Bill were so convincing in their evidence of events that they started to believe their own concocted story themselves and the more they relayed it the more they believed it to be the truth. It was as if Wilf had never pictured in the day's events at all, as if he hadn't played out his part, hadn't been responsible in any way for his brother's death. But, at the end of the darkest of days all three of them knew the truth of the matter and it was a truth that would not stay buried or silent forever.

As the funeral was taking place on Wednesday 9 July 1941 the local newspaper was preparing a column on the inquest into Kenneth's death conducted in an almost make-shift manner the day before, on Tuesday 8 July.

Wheels and formalities turned around very quickly during war years. A person could be dead and buried in the blink of an eye. Not too many questions were asked and therefore not too many answers needed to be given. At the exact time that Kenneth was being buried, together with the truth and the tears, the local newspaper was preparing and printing a report of the incident:

***

GOLDEN HILL BOY'S DEATH

An expedition by Golden Hill boys which ended tragically was described to the District Coroner at the Arclid Institution yesterday when he returned a verdict of 'Accidental Death' on Kenneth Hackney, aged nine, the son of Mr and Mrs William Alfred Hackney of John Street Golden Hill.

Kenneth was drowned in the canal at Red Bull on Saturday.

Evidence was given by Kenneth's father and mother to the effect that the boy left home about 2pm saying that he would 'only be a minute'. He went with some other boys, one of whom said he had been playing in Wilson's Wood: but a girl said she had seen him on the canal side. When the boy did not return in the late afternoon and early evening his father went to search for him. Later he identified the body at the Police Station.

DECIDED NOT TO TELL

A ten-year old boy said that they went with other boys to bathe in the canal. He got into the water first and

Kenneth dived in afterwards but he went under the water. The boy said that he got a stick to try and get him out and afterwards got dressed and left with another boy who had not been in the water. They caught up with some other boys who had been running and they all agreed that they would not tell anybody what had happened.

The Coroner: "That was an unkind thing to do. Why did you tell those lies about Kenneth being in the wood?

The boy: "My nerves went bad."

WAS FRIGHTENED

A nine-year old boy said he did not tell his Mother he was going to the canal. He told her he was going for a walk. Kenneth had a towel tucked beneath his jersey when he left the house.

Asked by the Coroner why he did not tell Mrs Hackney this he said "I was frightened".

Police Constable Shaw said that when he got to the bottom of the truth he entered the water and found the body on the bottom of the canal. It had been there for some time. He tried artificial respiration. Clothing and a school towel bearing the name 'Hackney' was found on the canal side.

The Coroner commended the action of the constable and the way he dealt with the matter. He went into the water to look for the body and found it.

***

It was however the detail that the report omitted to include that was by far the most distressing to hear. A fine white froth had been discovered in Kenneth's airways and slight haemorrhaging from one of his ears was noted. His stomach contained very little apart from what looked like desiccated coconut. His face and body were bruised. He had been lying face down, on the bottom of the canal for hours. Both of his hands were clenched, tightly closed, as if holding onto something precious. When, on the mortuary slab his clenched fists were prised open they were found to be full of debris and clay. It was therefore concluded that the boy had grasped in desperation at the sides of the canal in a vain attempt to save himself until he became exhausted and drowned.

CHAPTER SIXTEEN – THE TRUTH

WILF'S ACCOUNT OF SATURDAY 5TH JULY 1941

Kenneth asked if he could go out to play with a few of his school friends and Nell, without a second thought and a nod of her head gave quick approval. He winked at Wilf, smiled broadly and disappeared through the back kitchen door. It was a normal run of the mill Saturday morning and it would be one less for Wilf to watch over when Nell went out on her visit. When Bill had finished his shift at the Steel works, he planned as usual to go straight to one of the local pubs for a couple of pints of mild and a game of cards or dominoes. Only Wilf, Alma and Billy were at home in the house for most of the morning and all of the afternoon. Nell, with Terrence in arms left them just before noon to visit a woman whom she assumed was in some type of maternal need and who for fear of reproach had specifically asked her to be especially discreet. The last thing the woman in question wanted was for the village to get wind of her shameful state of affairs and automatically jump to the wrong conclusion. She had no option other than to trust Nell not to broadcast the facts of her unfortunate situation.

Besides, there were lots of British girls becoming GI brides although this woman, according to the rumours, was not expected to join their numbers simply because she was already married. The lass had wed a young man on a whim and a fancy before he'd taken himself off, just as soon as he'd got a ring on her finger, to fight in the war. Thankfully the young chap hadn't managed to put a bun in the oven before he'd left her. 'So what was she expected to do? Sit around twiddling her thumbs waiting for him or parts of him to be posted back home'. As a result of the gossip, and there had been plenty of that, Nell had more than an inkling about the reason behind the request for a visit and if her suspicions proved true then her administrations could take the majority of the afternoon.

The combined circumstances resulted in Wilf, the big 'un being left in charge of the house and his brothers and sister again. There was nothing at all unusual about the arrangement. It was, in fact, the most typical of Saturday mornings, and there was no reason whatsoever to suspect anything untoward would happen. Before Nell gathered up a sleepy-eyed Terrence out of the bottom drawer of the tallboy to take along with her on the visit, she pointed her finger into Wilf's face and reminded him, in no uncertain terms:

"Don't forget, if Mr Cooke knocks give him that sixpence off the shelf. I've left it separate from the rest of the copper. I didn't have any change to give him when he paid me with a shilling for his collars earlier so I told him to knock for it when he was passin'. He said he wouldn't bother and it would do for the collars next week but you never know he might think twice about it an' decide his sixpence would be safer in his pocket rather than in mine. Sixpence is sixpence and we could all be dead and bloody buried before this time next week so best to owe no bugger anythin'. Don't forget; give it to him if he knocks and remember to use your bloody manners when you do!"

As soon as Nell's back was turned Wilf set about raiding the tummy hole. He knew, from past experience, that his Mother's outings could last for hours and hopefully he would have plenty of time to raid, cook and clear away the evidence before she came home. He set to work walking spider-like again up the sides of the familiar pantry walls, unlocked the bolt and swung open the lid to the treasure trove. He stretched inside and grasped at a tin just within his reach. "Eureka! Fussell's condensed milk! What a catch!" He just needed some desiccated coconut to put with it. "Double Eureka!" he exclaimed as Alma and Billy, with eyes firmly fixed on their brother, echoed the word in unison. "Eureka" they shouted together, "Eureka". They had no idea at this point what their brother had actually discovered but assumed it must have been something good enough to eat and hopefully something sweet enough to savour. 'Woe betide him if Nell came back now' he thought. 'She'd wallop him so hard that he'd wonder what had hit him'. But, with condensed milk and a container of coconut in his hands he ignored all thoughts of a good hiding. Nothing would dissuade or deter him. Gravity eventually got the better of him and his feet hit the floor with a thud. Fortunately he had all he needed firmly grasped in both hands when the ceiling lid banged down on the secret store. He would have to remember to put the bolt on later or it would give the game away, Nell would smell a rat and before he knew it he would be in hot water up to his bloody neck again.

Followed closely by his two sibling shadows he hurried into the kitchen and heated up the stove. "No fear", he thought aloud, because "the oven would have gone cold again before his Mother returned. There'd be no evidence of anything and nothing would be outta place". He just hoped Kenneth would not miss the treat and be back in time to get more than his share of the coconut macaroons down his neck.

He worked like Billy-ho! No flies on him! He opened the back kitchen door as wide as he could to release the combined smell of baking and burnt bubbles of condensed milk cemented to the tray. He washed up and returned every bit of evidence of his misdemeanour back into its original place. Oblivious to his plan of action Alma and Billy started to chomp their way through the still warm macaroons.

"Leave some for ya brother" Wilf scolded, "and I dunna mean me. Leave some aside for our Kenneth and if yer see Mother coming through the back gate put what's left of 'em on the stairs as quick as you bloody can an' I'll hide 'em in the bedroom for a feast later tonight."

Luckily, there wasn't a sight, a sound or a sniff of Nell but neither was there any sign of Kenneth either. Wilf looked at the clock as it continued to tick away the minutes. Just gone one; he expected Kenneth back at anytime; 'bet he'd turn up starvin' hungry. So hungry that the macaroons would disappear in a bloody flash cuz he'd wolf 'em down two at a bloody time' he thought. Wilf could read his brother like a book and so refrained from eating any of his creations himself. He would wait to see how many of 'em his brother could manage to put away first. He could always have his share later assuming there was any left at all after his three siblings had taken their fill of them. It felt as if he was feeding the bloody five thousand without the luxury of five loaves and two fishes.

Wilf heard the latch go up on the back gate and immediately looked through the window worried it might be his Mother. Fortunately, it was Kenneth with three other boys who congregated at the bottom of the yard. His brother rushed into the house, through the back door and into the kitchen, alone. "How ya doin, our Wilf?" he nonchalantly asked. Quickly followed by, "Something smells good."

'So much for having destroyed and disintegrated the evidence' Wilf thought. He'd have to get rid of the smell by replacing it with another one and his only option might be a hefty measure of bleach or, failing that, a simple solution of bicarbonate of soda and water. Hopefully one of the desensitisers would do the trick and successfully eradicate the aromas of his covert culinary exploits.

"Wow! You've done us macaroons. You'll get what for if Mother finds out" Kenneth piped up whilst at the same time he picked up two or three of the roasted mini pyramids and made a good attempt at eating them all at the same time. He looked just like a hamster. His healthy red cheeks bulged with coconut and condensed milk.

"Well, she won't bloody find out, will she?" Wilf said raising his voice slightly in exasperation. "That is of course, unless some little bugger like you tells her and then you'll get what for as well for bloody eatin' 'em". They stared at each other for a few seconds until a big grin broke out across both of their faces. They burst into laughter together resulting in Kenneth spraying the kitchen with bits of coconut. "That'll teach ya" Wilf said. "Your eyes are bigger than your bloody belly!" Kenneth reached up to put his arm around his brother's shoulder as they scooped up the few remaining treats on their way through to the middle room.

Kenneth's playmates were waiting and hovering sheepishly at the bottom of the yard for their friend. "What are they up to?" Wilf enquired nodding towards the window. "They're just waitin' for me. We're off out together this afternoon" he replied. "Goin' swimming we are," he cheerily added. "Just need ya to give me that sixpence off the end of the shelf to tack with me. They've got theirs an' I just need mine and then we'll be off."

"No chance". Wilf raised his voice and continued. "Thait got no bloody chance. Thait got more chance a being struck by lightning! What do ya think our name is

Baron bloody Rothschild? Ya can go and tell 'em that you can't go with 'em. Sixpence for the swimming baths! There are more important things than that. Money doesn't grow on bloody trees."

"I'll do jobs for it. I'll pay the money back somehow. Aw, come on our Wilf. You know I like goin' the baths an' me Mother promised me I could go. It's so hot out there. Please, please just give us the sixpence. If you don't I'll just pick it up and tack it meself anyway" Kenneth implored.

"You bloody won't. The sixpence stays where it is and if you bloody touch it I'll cut your fingers off. I'm in charge and besides it's not mine to give thee. The sixpence stays where it is." Wilf firmly reiterated his order.

"Well how much copper is there then? Just count it out for us; there might just be enough. Look, I can see two pennies and a ha'penny among all that change. Aw come on our Wilf just give us sixpence. You've let me have copper before outta the change. That's what Mother leaves it there for. In case we need owt." Kenneth continued to fight his corner.

"Thait having none of it and that's the end of it. Silver, copper, bloody none of it. Swimming baths my arse. Don't ya think I'd rather go swimming instead of standing here sweatin' like a pig an' cooking coconut macaroons on a lovely sunny day? I've got no chance of doin' that and neither have you. Now go an' tell 'em that your Mother says you can't go with 'em and do as you're bloody told."

"But it's not fair. All the others have got sixpence. I only want sixpence. What's that to you? Come on our Wilf please let us have it. I won't tell Mother you gave it to me. Aw come on. Don't be such a spoil sport."

"No. The answer's No, No, No. Now don't ask again" Wilf shouted as he raised his hand to his brother in frustration.

With that Kenneth stomped on every step up to the top of the stairs and into the bedroom before coming back down 'em all faster than he went up. Little did Wilf know that upstairs his brother had stuffed his school towel with his surname embroidered in the corner under his jumper. He grimaced at Wilf as he passed him, banged the door and went outside to join the waiting boys at the bottom of the yard. It was the last time Wilf ever saw him.

CHAPTER SEVENTEEN –
RESHAPING THE PAST

"Can you begin to imagine what it must feel like to drown?" Wilf asked his daughter but did not wait or pause for an attempt at a response. He immediately, without taking a breath, started to answer his own question. He knew the answer only too well. The facts were ingrained into the depths of his body, mind and spirit.

"I do, he said, I learned about it. Drowning is suffocation due to immersion of the nostrils and mouth in a liquid." (He talked as if he was reading a section of a book memorised off by heart) "In our Kenneth's case the liquid being half the contents of the canal at Red Bull. Death from drowning is, I understand, complex and is not simply asphyxiation due to suffocation. Submersion is followed by a struggle during which time the person grasps for anything they can lay their hands on; twigs, debris anything at all they can grab. That's why our Kenneth's rigor mortised hands were full of clay. The lad had grabbed at the sides of the canal in blind panic. He couldn't swim, you know. In fact, he'd only been to the public baths a few times with the school. When the person becomes exhausted from the struggle, drowning begins and when the breath cannot be held any longer water is inhaled and the lungs start to fill. As the water goes in then coughing and vomiting start. Mercifully, I understand, and I hope to God it's true, this is followed by a loss of consciousness and death happens within minutes. After death, more often than not, the corpse lies face down at the bottom of what they've drowned in and that's why our Kenneth was discovered face down on the bottom of the bloody canal." After a pause and the deepest of sighs Wilf continued his own interrogation: "I've heard it said that their life flashes before 'em as they drown. I wonder if it really does and, if so, what our Kenneth saw? Anyway, who really knows the truth of it?" half answering himself. There was total silence in the room. How could the listener or anyone else in the world, for that matter, possibly respond; the words commanded reverence and respect.

Neither Wilf nor his wench reached for the light switch as the dimness of dusk slowly turned to darkness and seeped into the small living space. The room was overfull with its single bed and its on-loan recliner chair that had taken the place of his sky blue leather Frayling three-piece suite. Wilf felt as proud as punch of his sale-of-the-year bargain of a real leather sky-blue suite and regularly ruled the world from one of its armchairs. The wall space of the room became amass with photographs of his children, grandchildren and great grandchildren and yet was never completely full. He always had room for more and as his family grew the wall space seemed to grow with it. Every visitor to the flat, including nurses looked and listened intently as he explained to them who was who and who did what in life. It had truly become his personal wall of fame and yet there was no photograph of himself to be seen anywhere upon it. It was all about his children and his children's children. There was however just enough space amid the family portraits for a wall clock with a pendulum. Wilf had always had a clock in all the living rooms of all the houses he had ever lived in which served to remind him that time should always be valued and treasured. The clocks ticked away the precious seconds, minutes, hours, days, months and years and all time, whether short or long, was considered to be a gift and uniquely important. Once spent, time could never be regained or recaptured and so it was his practice to pack it with as much love and meaning as possible. It was considered a crime to waste it.

Wrapped in the silence and safety of all that Wilf held dear and within sight of the images of every one of his family the hands of time turned back the clock to enable the boy within him to relive the memories engraved on his heart. The day of Kenneth's funeral started to play across his mind and there was no pause or stop button to press as he retraced his steps to relive the day that was the culmination of his worst fears and failings and the ones that had haunted him for most of his life.

***

Without making a single sound, Wilf recalled the loss of his nine-year old Brother. He saw himself, almost twelve years old, falling in line behind Kenneth's coffin.

218

As instructed, he stood tall. Head up, shoulders back. He saw the ropes tightly wrapped around the bearers' hands and the small coffin, perfectly poised with just enough rope to allow it to swing between the four muscular men without touching the floor. He overheard his mother whisper to his Aunt that they hadn't had enough money to buy a shroud to wrap his brother's body in and he wondered what clothes, if any, his brother wore inside the darkness of the box that encased him. He watched the scene intently as he saw the neighbours quietly open and then quietly close their doors as they joined the family in Kenneth's final journey. He saw the posy of buttercups and daisies fall, in slow motion, off the centre of his brother's coffin. It hit the floor with what he thought was a reverberating thump before being crushed beneath the feet of the mourners as they continued their woeful walk to the chapel. He heard again the mellow tones of a tenor come from somewhere within the growing number of mourners as he started to sing the words:

"There's a home for little children, above the bright blue sky" and he remembered thinking that the sky wasn't blue, was it, not today, not even on this summer's day? It was grey, wasn't it?

Somewhere along the timeline of recollection, during the rerun of the funeral exactly as it had occurred years before Wilf ceased being an observer of the solemn scene. He no longer stood on the sidelines watching the day unfold and history repeating itself. He had somehow become the lad again and found himself actually walking, for a second time, behind the coffin of his brother. He was reliving the day's events all over again. Everything was exactly as it had been before and yet he was conscious that his mind-set was different, very different indeed. In fact, his thinking felt as sharp as a razor. Although physically a boy, a young lad, Wilf had somehow retained the knowledge and experience gained from his seventy-four years of life.

He was immediately aware of the strength of a youth's muscles and gasped as air filled his young lungs again enabling his breathing to become effortless and strong. He felt the sun on his stubble-free face and noticed his own shadow and that of his brother and sister fall behind them on the cobbled road. He felt more alive than he had in a very long time and, for an instant, he wondered if he had died. He glanced down at his shadow again and remembered from somewhere in his distant past that ghosts did not cast shadows. He was still in the land of the living and yet he was a boy again; a boy who knew the affirmation of a life well lived. His mind was crystal clear. He understood, in a blinding light, what he had not appreciated as a lad, the meaning and value of his life. It appeared to him as a panorama, an entire landscape picture within a split second of time. He not only saw the steps he was taking on that day but every step on every road he had walked on his journey through life. He saw his life in its entirety and, momentarily, in a cat's whisker, he knew it had been purposeful and that nothing was ever worthless or lost. As if everything and in particular, the most painful of things, were of immense value. He sensed he had been a small yet vital part in a much higher intent, a bigger plan and given sufficient time everything, even the things that had not been meant to happen, would somehow overlap and fit together in a miraculous multi-faceted pattern. A picture in which even the darkest colours and shades symbolising tragedies of every description, atrocities, accidents, chronic illnesses and premature deaths would ultimately find a place of purpose and rest in the immense canvas.

Wilf tried to explain as best he could, what had happened to him in that moment of heightened awareness. He likened the ultimate masterpiece he had seen to a glass that had been broken by hitting the floor and smashing into millions of pieces. It was completely shattered beyond repair, worthless and useless. Shafts and shards of glass were everywhere. He said that peoples' lives sometimes felt like that glass, broken into millions of splinters by the repercussions of unfair and unjust happenings and cruel, callous circumstances. He did not doubt the truth of the parallel simile because his life had been fractured since the death of his brother and living was never the same without him. In that gift of acute realisation, in an almost blinding light experience, Wilf saw every last splinter of glass recovered and reshaped to create a breathtaking priceless diamond. An invaluable treasure of far more worth and significance than it had ever been or would ever have become had it not been unintentionally broken. He said that in its reshaping the diamond acquired a depth of beauty that was extraordinary in every minute detail. It was difficult for him to verbalise his experience or put into words something that was inexplicable. He was conscious of every miniscule detail of his life and although reliving the saddest of all its days a ray of hope broke through the darkness to illuminate his soul and challenge his limited perception of life.

His almost out of the body experience had not taken up a second of time and did not pause his rerun of the day he was reliving and although he stumbled a little he quickly regained his stride behind the coffin of his brother just as he had sixty-three years before. To everyone else at the funeral it was the original day and no one was aware that Wilf was reliving it again. Just as he started to feel more surefooted his heart missed a beat. He momentarily froze. He saw Fear Herself for the first time in his life he actually saw her ugly distorted witch-like face and her black sinister slippery slimy silhouette. She had appeared from nowhere to grab his throat at exactly the same time as she had before when his Mother, without a pause in her step, looked over her shoulder and straight into his young eyes. Her threatening look said it all and her warning rang out just as loud and as clear as it had all those years before. Fear tightened her vice-like grip of his throat and snidely whispered in his ear: "No tears, you hear me, no bloody tears else I'll give ya somehat to cry for when we get back" as she smirked and pressed her long pointed finger nails into his young skin. He was weak and powerless in her grizzly grip.

His Mother's look was also enough to have turned a man to stone and a sure promise of severe retribution if he failed to comply with her command. Impulsively Wilf started to bite down on the inside of his cheek just as he had before. He focused again on the taste of blood as it started to seep through the gaps between his teeth to deter and distract him from crying. But on this day, the second time around, he had the reasoning and the strength of character of a good man. A man who had played the cards life had dealt him to the best of his ability and who suddenly realised that there were always choices in life's decisions. Nobody had to do anything they did not want to do. He saw Fear for what she really was and although he could not stop himself from feeling afraid he could choose to expose and overcome Her. He knew full well what the consequences of burying his tears would be. He had lived with them for almost all of his life.

Try as he may, he knew that he did not have the power or ability to change his part in the events that had brought them all to this dreadful day. No amount of pleading or bargaining could ever have changed that. There was nothing he could have done or said that would have been able to bring his brother back to life. He had begged to change places with him a million and one times. Plea-bargained with God to take him instead of his brother and if it had been possible to exchange places then it would have happened a long time before. Life was lived by universal rules and they were applied to everything and everyone. Water, like fire and so many other things, has the power to both sustain and destroy life. However, in an unexpected and very unlikely way Wilf's pleas and prayers were being strangely answered. His Mother had often told him that God works in mysterious ways, His wonders to perform. He had been given an incredible opportunity, a second-chance to change his memories of the most painful of days. He did not know how long the surreal situation would last but knew he would only be given the opportunity to change his part in it. With the lessons of a lifetime tucked firmly under his belt he would chose to alter the day's course for the better if he possibly could. He had been given a rare gift and he would not waste it as the funeral procession continued to make its way down the High Street towards the chapel doors.

Wilf chose not look away as his Mother's eyes pierced his very soul. He abruptly stopped himself from biting down hard on the inside of his cheek as Nell turned away to stare again at the coffin that contained her blonde curly haired lad.

At first, nothing seemed any different than it had been years before. To the unseeing eye nothing had changed. In fact, everything seemed a perfect repeat of Kenneth's funeral just as it had happened on Wednesday 9 July 1941. The growing number of mourners still softly sang the children's hymn "There's a home for little children above the bright blue sky". No one stopped walking. It seemed a faultless re-run, an exact replica of the day and yet something was very different. If nobody else could feel it Wilf certainly could. He could feel it in every bone of his young body. And then he realised what it was, it was he who was different. Nobody else and nothing else, just him and in that moment of acute realisation he blinked and a solitary tear escaped from his overfull eyes and started to trickle down his face. From a mixture of initial shock and overwhelming fear his small hand instinctively wiped it away as fast as he could and hoped beyond hope that no bugger had spotted it, especially his Mother. He started to bite down hard again on the inside of his cheek as Fear with her nose touching his and her stench filling his nostrils repeated her over-exaggerated goading: "No tears, you hear me, no bloody tears else I'll give ya somehat to cry for when we get back".

He would not cry. He dare not cry. He was too afraid to cry. And yet, quite unexpectedly, the heart and mind of a seventy-four year-old man who found himself, for a few moments in time, in his own almost twelve year-old body had a very different perspective. Hindsight was indeed a wonderful thing and Wilf had been given the rare chance to change, if he wanted to, his reactions and responses to his Brother's death. More than a little shocked and stunned by this realisation he questioned himself further. 'Had he not learnt anything from his life on this earth? His just over three score years and ten. Were tears really a sign of weakness? Was his Mother right in her stance regarding them especially tears for a lost brother and a lost son? Had he not read somewhere during his service in Korea that tears were counted and precious to God, so precious that He collected them in a bottle and numbered them in a book? So, if they were precious to God Almighty then that was the final word on the matter. Tears were precious, very precious indeed' he concluded. With the short silent interrogation over and without further ado, he slipped his left hand into that of his sister Alma and with his right hand he reached out and grasped the hand of his brother Bill and in half a whisper, he softly said, "It's alright to cry".

Once the words were out Wilf saw Fear lift up the corner of her thick black cape and hurl it up and over her face. In a split second as her cloak swirled in the air he gasped at the sight of its horrific lining. It was alive with countless terrifying trophies taken from equally countless victims. Trophies of every fearful description adorned and formed the lining of her cape like scalps hanging from the belt of an Indian brave. Gruesome effigies of every description clung to it alongside lost hopes, dreams and aborted ambitions. Her cape smothered her. She cowered as if in acute pain before vanishing abruptly and completely from the scene. Her power over him was broken and every link of her custom-made chain snapped. No longer afraid to cry for fear of retribution and with increased confidence Wilf filled his young lungs with air and prepared to speak out again. This time he raised his voice loud enough to ensure that both his brother and sister positioned on either side of him would be sure to hear him above the sound of the singing: "It's alright to cry. There's no shame in it" he more confidently declared.

Although initially dazed and more than a little afraid themselves both Alma and Billy heard their brother's words and immediately looked up into his young face. One glance was all it took for them both to see the most precious of tears glisten like diamonds in the sun as they rolled down the face of their big brave brother. A brother who at last was tasting freedom from the controlling grip of Fear who, on the first time round, had handed him a shovel to help him bury his tears deep inside his heart. In almost the same second of time, with renewed strength and a hunger for freedom, he took a deeper breath and courageously raised his voice loud enough to ensure that his words reached his Mother's ears: "It's alright to cry. There's no shame in it. Tears are precious but not half as precious as our Kenneth. I tell ya it's alright to cry", he sobbed.

In Wilf's second chance replay of the day's events if Nell heard her son's words she did not look round to acknowledge them. But neither did she turn round to scold him with a look of disapproval and a threat of punishment either. And yet she must have heard his words because it was not solely for his sake that Wilf had been given a second chance to change the events of the day. It had been for hers as well. It had been for his brothers, Billy and Terence and his sister Alma and their families. It had been for his future family, his children, his grandchildren and his great grandchildren. It had in fact been for all the children on all the photographs displayed on the wall of his living room and for the spaces waiting to be filled in between them. Perhaps Nell realised when she heard her eldest lad bravely shout out the words: "It's alright to cry. There's no shame in it. Tears are precious but not half as precious as our Kenneth. I tell ya it's alright to cry" that it was the truth of the matter and that there was no shame, weakness or embarrassment in showing the world, if need be, how much her blonde curly haired lad had been loved and how much his loss hurt.

At the end of the return to that most terrible of days Wilf had relived the worst memory of his life and amended it to become how he had always wanted it to be; a fearless expression of his love, grief and regret for the loss of his brother, his confidant and his friend.

***

After the events of that day, a day when a young boy's forbidden and buried tears had been exhumed Wilf was able to rationalise events with a clearer perspective and talked openly and honestly about his part in the most tragic trauma of his life. Had he given his brother sixpence, just over two pence in decimal currency, then he would not have drowned in the canal. That the sixpence in question had not been his to give never held much credence or sway in his recollection of the day. It was crystal clear to him. Had he given his brother the money and faced the consequences of doing so then Kenneth would have lived a full and meaningful life alongside him. His chair would never have been empty and his place within the family circle would have been secure. He would probably have married. At nine he joined in with the other boys when they teased girls in the playground at school. Undoubtedly he would have had a family and Wilf would have been the proudest of Uncles to his offspring. 'What if he had continued to draw and paint and what if he had become an artist of note? What if he had made it big time and all their dreams of grandeur would have come true? What if? What if? What if'? It

228

was not just the loss of a brother that hurt but the compounded loss of all he might have become that was so hard to bear. If only he had given him the sixpence, the cost of washing, starching and ironing a few shirt collars, he had so pleaded for that day. If, by some miracle, he could have stood in his brother's shoes, taken his place in the canal then he would gladly have done it and more in the hope of saving his life. But, as it was, he lived out his life as best he could bearing, be it misplaced the burden of responsibility and guilt for the drowning and loss of his younger brother.

After the death of Kenneth and for the rest of his life Wilf clung to those he loved like grim death always fearing their loss in some way shape or form and as a direct result he naturally became their protector and shield. He reasoned that his stubbornness had let his brother down and resulted in his death. He vowed that he would not be accused of ever letting any bugger down again and especially a member of his family. He had made a fateful mistake. 'Someone had to be to blame. Someone had to be called to give an account for what had happened. Didn't they? Accidents didn't just happen, did they? So it was his fault, wasn't it?' And yet, on the other hand, he reasoned and acknowledged that accidents do happen in life because life itself is fallible.

There were far too many unanswered questions, far too much guilt and condemnation for the boy inside the man to humanly bear. He decided, be it wrongly, at a very early age that his brother's death had been his fault. He was the last family member to have seen his brother alive and he could have changed everything that happened. After the passing of sixty-three years the pain of Kenneth's loss had not dimmed one iota and with the end of his own life well and truly within his sights he still missed and longed for his nine year-old brother as much as he always had and as much as he always would.

CHAPTER EIGHTEEN –
THE BEGINNING

It was early May 2004 and Wilf rested easy on what was to become his deathbed in the small living room of his housing association flat. Brenda, still his sweetheart, was too ill herself to help care for him but faithfully watched over him. She had her own unique memories of him and as she looked back over the years of their lives spent together she remembered how he had sung to her when she had been a young bride and pregnant wife:

'When your hair has turned to silver,
I will love you just the same.
I will always call you sweetheart,
that will always be your name'

and whatever else he had been, her faithful husband had been more than true to the sentiment of the song. She had been, was and would always be his sweetheart.

During the last weeks of his life his care fell to his six bairns, his three lads and his three wenches, and they rose to the mark and embraced the challenge of their lives as best they could. They were fortunate to be supported by both Marie Curie nurses and the local hospice at home team of professionals who proved invaluable in the situation.

Wilf, at times, appeared light-hearted as if relieved of a huge burden and whatever wrongs had been engraved on the slate of his life had somehow been eradicated, wiped clean. It seemed as if he was determined to make his peace, as far as possible, with God and man alike. He held up his hands often enough in recognition that not every bugger had liked his straight-laced manner and the fact that he called a spade a spade. In terms of views and opinions he undoubtedly held a very black and white perspective, right was right and wrong was wrong in his book with very few grey areas, if any, in between. It was as simple as that. He said that 'you stood for something or fell for anything and everything in life and he was always right even when he was wrong'. If any bugger crossed him or, worse still, crossed one of his own then they would probably live to regret it because he would go through 'em all like a dose of Epsom salts. He would have gone to hell and back for any of his children. Men and women alike always knew exactly where they stood with him and exactly what he was thinking or feeling.

He still enjoyed his daily wager on the horses and continued to wait patiently and expectantly for his hundred to one winner to come in. Needless to say it never did but that didn't stop him from hoping that it would. There was in fact a small part of him that had always fancied becoming a rich man. To have had the opportunity to have owned 'a big fine house with roofs by the dozen, right in the middle of the town' just like Tevye in Fiddler on the Roof. 'So what would have been so terrible if he had a small fortune?' Conversely, he never ceased to think it a treat to have the luxury of hot running water and thought it a pleasure and privilege to feel as warm as toast especially during the darkest of winter months. On one of his holidays in breath-taking Scotland he telephoned his family to tell them he was warm and that there was plenty of hot water in the hotel. He had seen first-hand and never forgotten the immeasurable amount of good that having enough money in life could do and the difference that having sufficient money could make to individual and family lives. For a start, he said, 'money could buy a uniform for the grammar school or any other school for that matter. It could put food on the table, clothes on the backs of children and shoes on their feet. Not to mention fancy cars and holidays abroad.' The world had certainly got smaller over the last few years of his life. One of his bairns, he boasted, had even travelled to the United States of America. 'How wonderful was that? The USA' he mused. How he would have loved to stand at the top of the Empire State Building. He regularly wondered if any of his ancestors had opted to emigrate from Ireland to North America to escape the potato famine and if so how they had fared. It was recorded that some immigrants who had been forced to go, were so poor that they had been stark naked on the coffin ships for the entire passage. Those who did survive the crossing had to be clothed by charity groups in America before they could leave the bloody ship. So, yes, Wilf appreciated the worth of wealth and having enough money to live on because he knew, only too well, what it was like to be poor, so poor that he genuinely had not owned a pot to piss in! Quite philosophically however, he remained wise enough to realise that, in so many ways, he was a very rich man indeed. His treasures, his family, were his lifelong investments and they were all simply priceless in his eyes and estimation. He remained confident that 'one day his investments, his sacrifices, would come home to roost and his boat would well and truly come in'. He would not have traded one of his kith and kin for all the Crown Jewels in the Tower of London put together. They were all beyond earthly worth and value and no bugger would ever have been able to put a price on any of 'em.

Still alive and kicking another great-grandchild was born to him at the beginning of April. As soon as he held her in his arms of blessing he formerly and officially declared her a real beauty, a stunner. He eagerly awaited the birth of his next one due at the end of May and the 'want-to-see-happen' date was clearly marked on his calendar. He would soon have children, grandchildren and great grandchildren coming out of his bloody ears and he loved it and every one of them equally. None of them was ever treated any differently than the other; they were all equal in his estimation and collectively combined to become the icing on his cake. He said that he could leave this life knowing that his family were doing well and had no worries for any of them. Even his wenches were forging their way in the world and leaving their marks in all types of professions like education, law and nursing.

'So much for thinking that they had their place in the home,' he joked. Cultures and traditions had changed quickly and women, including his own, were helping to change the world. Hopefully they would do a good job of it alongside, not in front or behind, but side-by-side with men of integrity and together they might narrow the gap between wealth and poverty, rich and poor. Wipe out the monsters of war, want and famine. Smooth out the playing field of life in an attempt to raise equality and stamp out all forms of injustice. 'But to do all that and more if they possibly could, one of 'em, at least one of 'em, would need to go into politics and even', dare he dream again, 'become Prime Minister'.

***

SATURDAY 15 MAY 2004

Wilf had received a blood transfusion at the local hospital and been discharged home to the care of his family in what was to become the last week of his life. He was entirely comfortable and taking no form of pain relief whatsoever.

Almost as soon as he saw his daughter early on Saturday morning and before she sat down next to him, he pulled back the bed sheet and light blue duvet cover and started to swing his legs out of the bed whilst at the same time issuing her an instruction: "Get me my suit. I need my suit". His feet by this time were both firmly on the floor.

"Why, where are you going, Dad?" she asked. "I'm going away with these honest men here. They're waitin'

235

for me" he confidently replied. His daughter did not need to look around the small living room but did so nonetheless simply because her Father was so convincing about what he could see before him. Needless to say there was no one else physically present in the room, no one, that is who his daughter with her twenty:twenty vision and earthbound eyes could see. "Not yet Dad" she instructed. "Please not yet" encouraging him back into bed.

"Are ya sure I conna go with 'em?" he asked. "Let me go. They're waitin' for me. Just get me my best suit outta the closet. They're honest men an' I dunna want to keep 'em waitin'" he insisted as his wench ignored his comments and covered him over with the freshly starched and ironed blue duvet cover. If there were men in the room with them then his wench did not want to see them. She did not want to acknowledge the presence of honest men or any other kind of men for that matter who wanted to take her Father away with them. She did not want it to be her Father's time to travel on without her and leave behind those he loved and those who loved him. It felt so unfair and if she had anything to do with it they, whoever they were, would have a bloody long wait to take her Father anywhere. She had only recently started to fully understand him, to completely and totally accept him, to get to know him as one knows a really good friend with all their foibles, inside out and back to front. It could not therefore be time for him to leave no matter how honest the men who were waiting for him were. 'No, he was staying put. She would make damn sure of

236

that. Get his best suit out! No bloody chance! He was going nowhere' she firmly concluded as she looked in defiance around the empty room.

Wilf was totally and completely coherent and not taking morphine or any kind of opiate and yet gave the impression of looking forward to going away as one would look forward to going on holiday with the best of friends. Friends, that did not criticise, judge or condemn but true friends who accepted and loved a person warts and all. He told his wench that although he thought life was far too short in its span dying would be just like going through a door into another dimension. He said he had seen the door but had not gone through it to look on the other side of it. On one occasion he talked, most unusually, about the crucifixion of Christ and in particular the nails that had been hammered into the hands of Jesus. He told her that he had talked with Him only the night before and that he had come to understand that the wounds in His hands and feet were in fact the marks of divine love. Over the last few days of his life Wilf became a true representation of the meaning of his Christian name Wilfrid, which is not only a saint's name, but in broader terms means Peace. He actually became a personification not only of the meaning of his name but also of his favourite word Shalom, the wonderful word that means so much more than peace in itself. In fact, a connotation of the Modern Hebrew word 'Shulam' may also be interpreted to mean 'fully paid'. Wilf owed no bugger anything and there wasn't a tear left in the buried bottle of truth that had haunted him for so many long years and often overshadowed his life. Fear was nowhere to be seen. A search with the finest of toothcombs would not have found her or any of her entourage. She could not be sensed in any part of the room. Having been left with nowhere to hide She had abandoned her mission in the face of mercy, forgiveness and love. Her accomplice Charon had gone with her and would not be receiving a payment for this man's final passage; it had already been paid for him in full.

In the early hours of Tuesday 18 May 2004, without any fear or foreboding, Wilf walked peacefully through the doorway that separated life from death. He had kept the honest men waiting long enough. He could not have resisted their invitation forever even though it had meant leaving behind the most precious, priceless 'things' that this temporal world afforded him, his family. If the honest men who were kept waiting in the wings were not all angels, then perhaps, just perhaps, one of them might well have been Kenneth, and, perhaps, just perhaps, as Wilf neared the door to eternity he felt a hand grasp his own and immediately two brothers, who had both suffered so much, stepped over the threshold together into a very different dimension. A place where their tears were completely wiped away and where united they would never again feel the pain of loving and losing someone they had so desperately wanted to keep.

***

Sometime after his death his eldest wench briefly visited her Father's graveside just a stone's throw from the orchard he had raided as a boy. As she stood for just a few short minutes reading the inscription:

WILFRID ROY HACKNEY

25.10.1929 – 18.5.2004

SHALOM

NIGHT AND GOD BLESS

on his gravestone two large butterflies landed simultaneously on her skirt. A butterfly had never landed on her before and yet in those few moments of quiet reflection two of them settled on her at exactly the same time. Immediately she recalled her Father's story of Sunrise and Sunset and the saying:

'What the caterpillar perceives is the end, to the butterfly is just the beginning'.

When she felt a tear roll down her face she did not wipe it away but heard herself say: "It's alright to cry. There's no shame in it. Tears are precious but not half as precious as Wilf and far too beautiful to ever be buried."

EPILOGUE

At times of logic Wilf reasoned that his brother's death could not have been solely his responsibility. He was after all only an eleven year-old boy when the tragedy happened. But, Guilt's destructive roots had burrowed so deep into his heart that he was unable to free himself from her clutches. He never allowed himself the indulgence of forgiveness until a higher authority bestowed it on him. After untold deliberations he always came to the same conclusion that someone must have been to blame for his brother's death so that someone may as well have been him as any bugger else.

WHAT ABOUT THE REPORT OF THE INQUEST?

It wasn't until later in life that Wilf found, hidden away at the back of a drawer in his parent's house, a newspaper cutting of an article reporting the Inquest into his brother's death. He read and reread the cutting before reading it again. He could not quite believe its account, as given at the end of Chapter Fifteen, even though he was reading the report in black and white and it was as clear and as plain as the nose on any bugger's face he still found what he read difficult to believe. The report was nothing short of a fabricated cock and bull story. Barely any of it was true. To start with, he had been left in charge of the house as usual on that fateful morning and had been the last one of his family to have seen his brother alive. Kenneth had returned to the house with some friends wanting sixpence to take him to the swimming baths and his decision not to give it to him resulted in his death. Wilf had thought more than once that he might just as well have flicked a coin into the air and allowed it to have decided his brother's fate. Heads Kenneth had the sixpence, tails he didn't. At least that way he could have blamed luck or the lack it for his brother's death. As it was he had always thought that he had been responsible and had decided his brother's fate by rolling the dice of misplaced responsibility and fear.

Nell and Bill were not in the house when Kenneth called home. His playmates all waited outside for him and did not see or hear Wilf and wrongly assumed that Nell was at home. Bill was in the Horse and Jockey and Nell was visiting a woman in need. Wilf's account of the mid-morning and afternoon of that day was as recorded in Chapter Sixteen. His parents, after Kenneth's death and during the blackest night made a pact to protect their bairns from as much unnecessary heartache and pain as they possibly could. They naively thought that their plan had worked and the truth, along with the tears, would remain buried forever.

The report of the Inquest said that Kenneth's friends had run away and left him. They were so afraid, so petrified they deserted him. Fear had obviously gripped their young hearts and overtaken their minds and reason.

She had been there waiting and watching as their playtime and fun went irrevocably wrong and after Kenneth had drowned She took firm possession of them all. Perhaps they were too afraid of the repercussions and reprisals of telling the truth from the off. Instead, in the face of Fear, they chose what they thought, in the short term, was the lesser of two very different evils and options.

What happened alongside the canal bank that afternoon did not die a death and after the inquest rumours rumbled around the village for a very long time. One rumour in particular recounted that someone had, in fact, pushed Kenneth into the canal. It was suggested there had probably been some clowning around and showing off on the canal side. Kenneth could not swim and may even, when it came down to jumping in, have chickened out and, in playful mood, been pushed in just for the fun of it.

The only thing the Inquest report was one hundred per cent accurate about was the verdict of 'Accidental Death'. No one person including Wilf, or a group of people including his playmates had been responsible for Kenneth's death. It was a tragic accident. Nothing was intentionally or deliberately done to cause his demise.

Kenneth himself had not been to blame. He was totally innocent, a nine-year boy having fun on a summer's afternoon. His friends were not to blame. They had simply been playing together on a warm July day. PC Shaw and Sergeant Pierce had asked them all the obvious questions and been satisfied with all of their answers. The boys, including Kenneth, had chosen to cool off in the canal and the truth of what happened would never be fully known. But, one thing remained a certainty the tragedy was not anyone's fault. It was not Kenneth's nor any of his pals, not Nell's or Bill's, not even James Brindley's for designing and building the canals, not God Almighty's, although he would do if there was nobody else to pin it on and finally, it was not an eleven year-old brother's fault who made a decision based on obedience and fear. It had been an unintentional heart breaking misfortune and an accidental death epitomised it perfectly.

WHAT ABOUT RESPONSIBILITY?

Children can carry transferred, assumed or delegated responsibility which does not belong to them. Responsibility that has inadvertently been placed on them or that they have somehow absorbed and taken on board themselves. Perhaps if we could imagine it as a big heavy wet blanket draped across their shoulders then surely we would rush to relieve them from its burden. Lift it off their shoulders and set them free. But, because it cannot be physically seen, although its effects can easily be detected, it somehow remains hideously heinously hidden. It need not be the death of a sibling that results in an overbearing sense of responsibility or life-long guilt that weighs heavy across the heart and shoulders of a child. Children often feel responsible for all kinds of things including the breakdown of family relationships, births and sadly deaths. The impact and repercussions behind the story of 'Buried Tears' not only touched the lives of its main characters but also in many ways reshaped them. Wilf loved children and if one child, however old, can be set free from the burden of misplaced responsibility as a result of reading his story then it would have made the telling of it worthwhile. He often said that children can only become what we enable them to be and therefore we must believe and trust in them because if we don't then who will?

WHAT ABOUT GUILT?

We all at some point in our lives open the door to Guilt and invite her in. We all fall short of standards especially moral ones. There are innumerable markers, rulers, expectations, far too many to mention and far too many to attain. Yet consciously or subconsciously, covert or blatant they exist and we use them to measure ourselves and unforgivably to measure others by. In some circumstances we sentence ourselves, and others, by acting as judge, jury and even executioner. We pass sentence without knowing the facts, without walking a mile in the other person's shoes. We may have looked to religion and only discovered more markers. Within all faiths there can be different interpretations, variants of laws and levels of understanding, endless standards and rules that are often bent to suit and fit a purpose or accommodate changing lifestyles and patterns. In our arrogance, we measure ourselves by feeble interpretations of tenets, doctrines, standards and expectations and pronounce ourselves and others guilty. Wilf knew exactly what Guilt was like because he lived with her sitting on his shoulder alongside Grief and Fear for the majority of his life until he experienced during his final days the gift of grace and forgiveness from the hand of mercy. He said he could see honest men waiting for him. Hopefully they were honest enough to tell an eleven year-old boy that no matter how close to twenty-one he felt he had not been responsible for his brother's death.

WHAT ABOUT FEAR?

If we do not control and master Fear then make no doubt about it, She will control and master us. It is possible however to use her own power against her. To turn it upside down and inside out by transforming fear into courage and denying her the satisfaction of adding another trophy to the lining of her cape. Perhaps we could learn to harness her and make her submit to our autonomy, refusing to allow her to rule the roost. Wilf said he thought one antidote to her taunts was Faith and coupled with Love and Hope her poison could be diluted and nullified. It is not just about living on the highs of life that is important but working through the fearful lows and dross of the valleys that often stretch and shape us. Discovering the courage to eyeball our deepest fears, fighting them back and overcoming them determines and defines our nature before leaving the deepest of imprints on our heart. Given sufficient time such victories especially over fear strengthen our character enabling us to reach out and touch the lives of others. As a result, not only do we deny Fear her trophies of aborted dreams and destinies but, more importantly, we amass trophies of our own. Faith is an antidote to fear but one not necessarily found in fallible doctrines but rather in the hearts of those who will simply believe.

WHAT ABOUT GRIEF?

There are some things, like Grief, that touch all lives and all faiths including atheism. The fact is that none of us run through the valley of the shadow of death. We walk through it one arduous step at a time. Sometimes one-step forward and then many back. We can try to take short cuts over the top of the valley to avoid her shadows but suppressed effects will somehow, somewhere show themselves by weaving their way into our relationships before seeping into every area of our lives. It might help us to remember that they are only shadows we try to bypass and not actual substance and where there is shadow there must also somewhere be light. Valleys can be beautiful places if we take the time to walk gently through them, learn what they have to show us and absorb their reality. Afford ourselves the luxury of a respectable mourning period and wear a black satin ribbon around the confines of our hearts and lives until we feel ready and able to release it ourselves. Grief is a natural response and reaction to the unique experience of loss and the resultant excruciating pain it can cause. It takes an immense amount of courage to acknowledge and accept Grief and eventually learn to respect and even embrace Her. She has the rare ability and compassion to transform pain into acceptance and eventually into peace or, as Wilf would have said, Shalom. As he discovered towards the end of his life there can be healing in Grief's tears no matter how long they have been buried for.

IS IT THE END OR IS IT THE BEGINNING?

Generally speaking, we have been programmed to expect fairy tale endings to all of our stories and situations. In reality this idea falls far short of real-life experience and often leaves us feeling robbed or short-changed. Wilf, it could be said, was not actually the last person of the family to have seen Kenneth. Nell was adamant that she saw him on the day he died just before Bill arrived home after identifying his body at the police station. She recounted that she was sitting in her rocker just watching the clock and waiting when she saw Kenneth as plain as day walk through the house hand-in-hand with her Mother who had died a few years earlier. From that eerie moment she knew, before Bill told her, that her blonde-haired boy was dead to this world but was comforted by the fact she had seen him leave it holding the hand of someone she loved and trusted.

When a pebble is thrown into a lake the ripples of water caused may take many detours before reaching the shore. Our lives, however short or painful, release ripples that somewhere somehow touch the lives of others. They tend to travel at their own pace and may take a very long time before reaching their final destinations. In Kenneth's case the ripples of his life have taken over seventy years to surface and have at last started their journey. The story of his young life, accidentally cut short, will now begin to touch the lives of others before finally reaching the shoreline. It is not, after all, the quantity of pages contained in a book or the length of days in a life that counts but rather the quality of what has been written on the pages and lived out in the days that can make an ultimate difference. The fact that we do not own anyone however much we love them, that they do not belong to us, like an adornment or possession encourages us to value their one-off uniqueness. Everything we can see with our natural eyes is temporal but the unseen things, like love and the soul itself, is eternal. So is it the end or is it the beginning? Love has built a bridge across time into eternity and when linked with Faith and Hope has the power to transform death, often perceived as the end, into life, which is just the beginning.

The final word in the book belongs to
Wilf and is, of course,
Shalom.

A SELECTION OF FAMILY PHOTOGRAPHS
FROM THE AUTHOR'S PRIVATE COLLECTION.

Bill, Nell and their depleted brood. (1946)

'The Cake' 16 December,1950.

'The Wedding Party' 16 December, 1950.

**Waiting for my Father to come home from Korea
John Street, Goldenhill. (1952)**

On the Chapel Steps.

ACKNOWLEDGEMENTS

My sincere thanks go to my family and friends for their endless encouragement, support and proofreading and especially to those closest to me who shared my dream and never stopped believing in my ability to make it a reality.

Thank you to the professionals and particularly In-Scribe, who helped me on my publication journey and last, but not least, thank you to my readers who have made the telling of 'Buried Tears' immensely worthwhile.

I will always feel proud of my upbringing and especially of being affectionately remembered as one of Wilf's wenches.